Two days after Capone returned to his power base another man took a train to Chicago—this one from Washington, D.C.

He was a tall, lanky man in his early thirties. He had a strong-boned face inherited from his Norwegian parents. His eyes had the expression of someone who looked at people and measured what he saw.

His brown three-piece suit, while not shabby, was three years old and looked it. When new, you could have bought a dozen like it for less than the price Al Capone paid for any one of his suits.

The .45 automatic pistol he sometimes wore in a shoulder harness under his left arm was packed away inside his suitcase. But he wouldn't be going anywhere without it after he reached Chicago.

Because his mission there was to smash Al Capone.

His name was Eliot Ness.

THE
UNTOUCHABLES

A novel by
MARVIN ALBERT
Based on a screenplay
written by
DAVID MAMET

IVY BOOKS • NEW YORK

Ivy Books
Published by Ballantine Books
Copyright © 1987 by Paramount Pictures Corporation. All Rights
Reserved.
Cover art copyright © 1987 by Paramount Pictures Corporation. All
Rights Reserved.

Library of Congress Catalog Card Number: 87-90782

ISBN 0-8041-0161-2

Manufactured in the United States of America

First Edition: June 1987

ONE

On the first day of September in 1930 Alphonse Capone boarded a luxury train in Florida and headed back to Chicago.

During that trip he expounded his thoughts on various world problems, and on life in general, to a reporter he'd invited along. The reporter appreciated the opportunity. An exclusive interview with Al Capone was surefire newspaper fare for thrill-hungry readers.

But the reporter was careful how he phrased certain of his questions. He was also careful not to report *all* of the antics of Capone's large entourage during that long train ride.

He wasn't eager to irritate Capone, who was a complex fellow. A brute, maybe—but not a simple one. For one thing, Al Capone liked to be liked. He hated having anyone not like him. The reporter never let himself forget how very many men had gone to early graves so that Big Al would not be irritated by their walking around disliking him.

Al Capone had turned thirty-one that year. He'd become a fat man by then. A big round body joined by a thick neck to a big round head. His face was round, too. With thick dark-colored lips and dreamy long-lashed eyes, and unpleasant knife scars on the side of his face he never let anyone photograph.

Some people said he looked like a grotesque clown. Flatterers said he looked a lot like the opera singer Enrico Caruso. There was no shortage of flatterers by 1930. By then he'd become "The Big Guy." Nobody bigger—in any mob-run city in Prohibition America.

His visit in the sun with his wife and son, at his Palm Island estate, had been a short one. Of necessity. He could never stay away from Chicago too long. His physical presence, and other people's fear of it, was the only thing that could hold together the vast criminal-political-business empire he'd constructed—from a bootlegging base—with his powerhouse strength, exceptionally clever brain, and legions of gunmen.

And with the help of the national Prohibition law.

At age thirty-one, Al Capone was now at the very height of his fortune, power, and fame—raking in hundreds of millions of dollars a year from his assorted rackets and his growing grip on legitimate businesses.

He was also, he noted regretfully whenever he looked in the mirror, at the top of his weight—from an unquenchable appetite for food and liquor. Capone now weighed almost 250 pounds. Sixty pounds more than when he'd made his first train trip to Chicago—from New York that time, just over a decade ago—to go to work for Johnny Torrio as a general strong-arm man and enforcer.

His meteoric rise since then Capone attributed, in part, to his ability to learn from other men.

From Big Jim Colosimo, for example, who had been the most successful racket leader in Chicago when Capone arrived there, Capone had learned the ways of high-level political graft and the uses of careful book-keeping. Big Jim was unfortunately no longer around. He'd been unwilling to change with the times. Unable to envision that Prohibition was going to make bootlegging a much more profitable business than whorehouses.

Johnny Torrio had regretfully confided his feeling that Big Jim was standing in the way of progress—to nobody else but young Al Capone. And Colosimo had died of three bullets in the ornate lobby of the best restaurant in town.

From Torrio, also unfortunately no longer around, Capone had learned how to grow through organization: uniting formerly rival gangs for mutual advantages. It was also from Torrio that he had learned the uses of charm. Capone hadn't had much of that when he'd first come to Chicago. He had a lot of it now. Acquired charm; but it had become as genuine, after the years of use, as the acquired fat.

It didn't cause many people to get foolhardy enough to treat Capone with any less fear and respect.

He had killed men with his fists, as well as club and gun. He still could, when the occasion demanded, or when the volcanic temper underneath the layers of fat and charm erupted out of control. Then the fat man could suddenly become an astonishingly swift and totally destructive force.

That didn't happen often anymore. Capone had an army of torpedoes and strong-arms to handle that kind of violence for him. But the potential was always there, inside this fat smiler, and the reporter interviewing him on the train trip from Florida to Chicago was careful not to forget it.

So the reporter, whose name was Larry Earl, phrased each question with forethought, making sure he didn't offend.

"Al," he said cautiously, "You don't seem to spend

much time with your wife and kid down there in that
Florida place you bought."

Capone sighed sadly. "That's the truth. I sure wish I
could be with them a lot more. I'm crazy about that boy
of mine, y'know. But I got too much work pressure waiting for me, and it's hard to concentrate on business with
a family around. You know how it is."

"Yeah, I know. Got a wife and kids of my own."

Capone smiled. "There y'are! So you do understand.
Work and family. A bad mix, eh? And me, I got too many
business responsibilities these days. That's what I am
now, you realize. A businessman."

"A *big* businessman," Larry Earl said.

"Right. A tycoon, you could say. Not some kind of
bum, like a lot of people go around saying about me."

"*I've* never said it."

"Because you're smart. Reporters understand things,
that's why I love 'em. You know what? That's what I
would've wanted to be if I'd had the education. A reporter."

"You wouldn't like the pay, Al."

"Yeah," Capone sympathized, "that's the problem,
ain't it. You guys don't get paid what you deserve.
That's why I like to help some of you out now and
then.... Say, are you a drinker?" Capone grinned and
answered the question himself: "Sure you are. All reporters drink. That's another reason I love 'em."

"I've been known to nibble a few," Larry Earl admitted.

Capone looked to the big bodyguard standing in the
doorway of his compartment, Tony Accardo. "Tony, go
get us a bottle of that cognac I just got in from France."

"Sure, Al." Accardo went off along the train corridor,
leaving two other bodyguards stationed just outside the
compartment door. There were more of those, out of
sight in compartments on both sides of Capone's. Tough
cookies like Louis Campagna and Phil D'Andrea. And

Frankie Rio, who'd saved Capone when his Cicero headquarters had been hit by eight carloads of machine-gun squads led by Hymie Weiss and Bugs Moran, trying to extract revenge for the murder of their beloved leader, Dion O'Bannion.

Since then Capone never went anywhere without a lot of guards around him.

The rest of this train carriage was filled with the rest of the Capone entourage: some of his closest lieutenants, assorted gorillas, and a number of the prettiest girls Larry Earl had ever seen. Most of the girls were for the amusement of Capone's hoods. But the two niftiest-looking ones were reserved for the boss himself. Al Capone had never lost the taste for whores he'd acquired as a seventeen-year-old bouncer in a Brooklyn brothel.

"You just spoke of yourself as a big business tycoon," the reporter resumed, choosing his words. "Aren't you actually much more than that? What I mean is . . . well, take an article I read in a New York paper a couple months ago. Somewhat sardonic, shall we say, but not entirely kidding, either. The article asked why, since it would seem that you are, in effect, the mayor of Chicago, why haven't you simply been *appointed* to that position, officially?"

Capone laughed heartily. "Yeah, I read that one. It was funny. Great sense of humor. . . ."

He was interrupted by Accardo's return with a small opened crate and two brandy glasses. The crate bore the red pine-tree emblem of a large, respectable Canadian liquor distributor.

Capone reached into the crate and pulled a bottle of cognac out of its bed of straw, showing Larry Earl its label. The reporter whistled appreciatively.

Capone liked that. "Like I said, the real stuff. All the way from France. Nothing but the best." He gave the bottle to Accardo, who began the job of respectfully opening it. Then he turned back to Larry Earl, and to the article suggesting he be named mayor of Chicago.

"Well, you know, I'll tell ya, that article was *touching*. Like a lot of things in life. We laugh because it's funny, and we laugh because it's true."

The reporter recognized the tone: Capone in a deep philosophical mood.

"Some people say," Capone went on, "people who call themselves reformers say, 'Put that man in jail, what does he think he's doing?' Well, what I hope I'm doing —and here's where that newspaper article's got a *point* —is this. What I'm doing is, I'm responding to the will of the people."

Tony Accardo poured generous amounts of cognac into the two glasses. He gave the first to Capone, the other to the reporter. Larry Earl took a sip of his and made a happy face. Capone grinned and took a large swallow from his own glass before resuming his speech.

"Now, there's some people who get upset and talk about me having disrespect for the law. But what the hell *is* law? Nothing but a reflection of the will of the people. Right? And in this case—in the case of Prohibition— well, it's a *bad* law. Because it does *not* reflect the people's will."

Larry Earl cautiously edged closer to what he really wanted to ask: "It's been written that the best way to do away with a bad law is to enforce it. Is Prohibition being enforced?"

Capone shook his head, almost sadly. "No. I'm not telling tales out of school when I tell you, Not really. And why not?" Capone gestured at the reporter's brandy glass with his own. "Because people *are* gonna drink. *You* know it. *I* know it. And all I do is *act* on that fact of life. So where's there anything bad in that?"

He finished off what was in his glass and resumed as his bodyguard refilled it. "And all that talk about lawless bootleggers—well, what *is* bootlegging? What's it mean?

In the back streets and cheap gin mills they call it bootlegging. In a ritzy mansion they call it 'hospitality.' So what am I doing, outside of selling the people what they want to buy? What does that make me, eh? Just a businessman. Like somebody selling cars or clothes. Supply and demand—that's what makes America the greatest and richest country in the world, everybody knows that. Am I right?"

Emboldened by the brandy, Larry Earl chanced the big question: "What about your reputation, Al? What people say about you controlling your business by violence? That those who don't purchase your products—or try to sell their own without your permission—get dealt with brutally?"

He was relieved to see that Capone did not appear to be offended.

"I grew up in a tough neighborhood in Brooklyn," Capone told him blandly, with a little smile. "We used to say in that neighborhood, You can get further with a kind word and a gun that you can with just a kind word."

The reporter laughed dutifully.

Capone's own laugh boomed in the confines of his elegant compartment. Then, abruptly, his expression became serious. He leaned forward and stabbed Larry Earl's knee with a thick, hard fingertip. "And in *that* neighborhood," he said pointedly, "it might have been true. And what happens is, sometimes a reputation *follows* you. Something from way back when you were just a dumb kid—and people try to pin the label on you a long time later, after you've changed into a sensible, responsible businessman."

Capone sighed dramatically and shook his heavy head. "There *is* violence in Chicago, Larry, sure. But not by me. And not by anybody that *I* employ. I wouldn't stand for it. And I'll tell you why not. Because it's *not good business*. And you can quote me on that!"

Larry Earl was not some naive cub reporter. He had

been around a long time, and he didn't have much trouble recognizing when he was being handed a large pile of horse manure. But he did intend to quote Capone, in full; and he was quite certain his newspaper would give it front-page coverage.

For the press, the guideline to what its readership wanted to be fed had been laid down clearly by its cynical sage, H. L. Mencken: "Nobody ever went broke by underestimating the intelligence of the American public."

That great newspaper-reading public would eagerly gobble up every word from the lips of this inflated thug. Because Capone's lordship—over not only Chicago but the entire era of Prohibition—had reached a point where he was no longer regarded as merely a successful gangster. He was a worldwide celebrity. People who had trouble remembering the name of the current President of the United States knew this man's name.

You could say the word "America" to people in Europe during this period of history and that was probably the first name that would pop into their minds: Al Capone.

Two days after Capone returned to his power base another man took a train to Chicago—this one from Washington, D.C.

There was no entourage traveling with him. Only his pregnant wife, Catherine, and their eight-year-old daughter. And about as much baggage as they could handle between them.

No reporters saw this man off or came along to ask his views on national problems. His name wouldn't have meant anything at all to the newspaper-reading public at that point.

He was a tall, lanky man in his early thirties, with hands that looked as though they would be good with tools. He had a strong-boned face inherited from his Norwegian parents. A quiet-spoken man with nothing exceptional-seeming about his appearance to cause other passengers to devote any special attention to him.

There were, however, some things about him that most wouldn't notice. His eyes, for example. They had the expression of someone who looked at people and measured what he saw. Nothing intimidating in that look. Just thoughtful.

And the long mouth could, on occasion, get a hard, eager set to it. Like it had now, as he stared out the train window at the passing scenery while Catherine read a children's story to their daughter on her lap. You could sometimes spot that same kind of look on a tough defensive end when he was planning to bust through the opposition line and smear its quarterback into the ground—the hard way.

His brown three-piece suit, while not shabby, was three years old and looked it. When new, you could have bought a dozen like it for less than the price Al Capone paid for any one of his suits.

And the jacket unbuttoned over this young man's vest was not a perfect fit. It was a half size too big for him.

That was so the .45 automatic pistol he sometimes wore in a shoulder harness under his left arm wouldn't show.

It wasn't there now. It was packed away inside his suitcase.

But he wouldn't be going anywhere without it after he reached Chicago.

Because his mission there was to smash Al Capone.

His name was Eliot Ness.

TWO

Frank Nitti stood just inside the entrance of the Lexington Hotel, Capone's Chicago headquarters, waiting for the driver to bring the car around the front. It was September 14, shortly after 2:00 P.M. The stubby fingers of his left hand gripped the handle of a bulging brown-leather briefcase. He held it very carefully, not moving it any more than was strictly necessary.

Nitti was an ugly man: flat-nosed, thin-lipped. The expensive tailoring that had gone into his blue serge suit included special reinforcement of the right-hand pocket. That was where he sometimes carried one of his weapons: the short-barreled .38 revolver. His hat was a soft pearl-gray fedora with a narrow black hand. By this tenth year of the bootleg era, that had become almost uniform among the torpedoes of Al Capone's army, with half the other hoods around town copying the style.

The eyes shadowed by the brim of Frank Nitti's fedora were pale gray with dark flecks in them, and had seldom been observed to reveal anything recognizable as a human emotion.

If those eyes had been capable of expression they might have shown, at that moment, a lack of pleasure in the weather waiting for him outside the hotel. Nitti had been imported to Chicago from the same brutal Brooklyn neighborhood as his boss. The weather back there hadn't been anything to sing about, either. Summers too hot and winters too cold, just like here. But at least New York didn't have the wind blasting across the lake out of Canada.

Chicago—the Windy City. This afternoon the wind was cold—and wet. The rain slanted before its force, big drops chasing each other furiously along street and sidewalks, building into churning streams in the gutters of Michigan Avenue.

Frank Nitti didn't like to work in the rain. But Capone had given him a job to do. And Nitti had never failed the Big Guy yet. Not all the assignments involved simple killings. Others required more subtle forms of problem solving. Knowing how and when to use bribery or blackmail, or a combination of both. Or leaning against stubborn characters with exactly the right tone of voice.

Whatever, Nitti could handle it. A reliable worker. Prompt, efficient, no mistakes. That was why Al Capone had come to depend on him as the best enforcer in his current stable.

So good that his job had become the nickname given to him by the underworld: Frank "The Enforcer" Nitti.

And that was why Nitti knew there was no limit to how high he could climb in this rich, violent, thoroughly corrupted town. All he had to do was to continue handling every job just right for his master. Nitti never forgot that this was exactly how Capone himself had begun his rise to the top of the heap—carrying out these same kinds of jobs for Johnny Torrio. Using whatever it took: a club, a gun, a bomb, or a quiet word in the right ear.

A tan LaSalle sedan pulled to the curb in front of the hotel. Nitti didn't run to it, in spite of the slashing rain. That wouldn't have been smart, considering what he was carrying.

He walked, stepping easy and letting the wet hit him, and made sure the briefcase didn't bump against anything when he got in beside Shelly Brennan, the driver. He balanced it on his knees before shutting the door. Then he gave Brennan the address: a speakeasy across the river on the North Side.

As the car headed for it Nitti raised the briefcase slightly with both hands and continued to hold it that way, to protect its contents from any ruts in the road along the way.

The assignment Capone had entrusted to Nitti that afternoon was an old-fashioned kind of job, almost outmoded in Chicago these days. But in the earlier years of Prohibition it had been an almost daily occurrence.

When the federal law against supplying or consuming liquor had gone into effect, a decade ago, Chicago's underworld was run by a number of independent neighborhood gang lords, with each gang controlling one small section of the city. The O'Bannion gang running the Northeast Side. The Genna family on the South Side. The Polish mob in the Southwest Side. Ragen's Colts in the Stockyards District. A dozen others.

Of course there had always been sporadic fighting between these local gangs. Attempts to cut into a rival's rackets and territory while protecting one's own. But nothing like the all-out warfare that erupted with Prohibition.

The new law handed the underworld an opportunity to make fortunes never even dreamed of before, through illegally catering to the citizenry's tabooed thirst. The incredible wealth and power a mob leader could acquire, if he could succeed in enforcing his control beyond the limits of his former slice of the city, was just too much to resist.

The most lucrative and hurtful targets were a competitor's breweries, major stills, warehouses, and liquor convoys. But these were hard to find and heavily guarded. That left the rival's speakeasies: the illicit saloons he owned or controlled. There were thousands of speaks scattered all over the city. Impossible to protect them all. So the speakeasies had become the prime targets. The only thing a booze baron could do about it when one of his speaks was hit was to strike back—as swiftly and viciously as he could.

In six years, it was estimated, some four hundred underworld hoodlums were slaughtered in this bootlegger war.

But that was in the past. Killings were still necessary, naturally. But less frequent, because less often needed. The years of all-out warfare had accomplished the objective. The weaker or unluckier of the old mob leaders had been put out of business: buried or scared into running for their lives.

The same was happening in every city in the country. Gradually, underworld power was coming under the control of a few of the strongest and smartest.

But nowhere like in Chicago.

Nowhere else, as yet, had one single gangster achieved total control of an entire city, as Alphonse Capone had managed to do in Chicago—through the wholesale slaughter of his competitors and the massive bribery of politicians, judges, and the police.

Which didn't mean that a complete peace reigned in Chicago under his domination. There were still minor irritations from time to time. Occasionally some discontented underworld hotheads would get together with a notion about how to grab themselves a bigger chunk of the action and kick the king of Chicago off his throne.

The latest attempt had been organized by a Sicilian

racketeer named Joey Aiello, together with his brother and a cousin named Benny Russo. Uniting with scattered and shattered remnants of the old Genna and O'Bannion mobs, they began to move in on the city's Sicilian strongpoints formerly run by the Gennas. Joey Aiello pointed out that Capone, being of Neapolitan descent, didn't have any right to tell Sicilians what to do. Capone sent out hit squads to disagree with him.

Outgunned, Joey Aiello tried to bribe the owner of the Little Italy Cafe to poison Al Capone's food. But the owner balanced the opposing forces in his mind and quickly informed Capone. Joey went into hiding and issued a contract: fifty thousand dollars to anybody who knocked off Capone. Finding Joey Aiello and company became the number-one priority of the entire Capone organization—including the cops on Capone's pad.

Joey's brother was located first, by Frank Nitti and Machine-Gun McGurn. They left him twenty-eight bullets heavier. It was Nitti alone who found and killed Joey Aiello. The surviving remnants of the O'Bannion and Genna gangs went back to being scattered and shattered. That left Joey Aiello's cousin, Benny Russo.

But Benny slipped out of Chicago and took off for parts unknown. That was all right with Capone. Benny, on his own, was not tough enough to lead any retaliation attempt. However, Capone didn't want Benny back in Chicago, ever. One way to make sure of that was to see to it that Benny didn't have anything to come back to. The only thing of value Benny had left in Chicago was a string of seven speakeasies. In Benny's absence they were being managed by his wife.

Capone went to see her, personally. She had nothing to fear. One of the strictest mob rules, in those relatively innocent times, was that noncombat members of their families must not be hurt. Alphonse Capone adhered passionately to that rule. He had a family of his own. A wife he kept tucked away most of the time at his Palm

Island estate in Florida, together with their son, whom he adored. So he didn't threaten Benny's wife. He asked her politely to get word to her husband that he wanted to buy up his speakeasies.

Al Capone was known to be a generous man, a soft touch for people having a hard time making ends meet. Ask any of the hopeful hangers-on around the lobby of the Lexington Hotel: the Big Guy's heart was as warm as his smile. It was not unusual for him to hand a beggar five bucks or pay a newsboy fifty for a single copy of a paper. He'd sometimes tuck a thousand-dollar bill in the pocket of some has-been nightclub comic or washed-up singer. The charm with which he accepted thanks made the lucky recipient feel the favor was mutual.

But Capone's generosity didn't extend to people who'd bucked him.

The price he offered for Benny's seven speakeasies was less than what any one of them was worth.

That had been more than a week ago. Benny had still not responded to the offer.

So Capone had given Frank Nitti a job to do. One perfectly suited to The Enforcer's talents and temperament.

THREE

It was a run-of-the-mill speakeasy in a run-down neighborhood. The population in these blocks was mostly unskilled laborers and their families, all having an increasingly difficult time getting by as the Depression, heralded by the Wall Street crash a year back, spread throughout every part of the nation.

This speak was the least profitable of Benny Russo's string of seven. Naturally, Capone wanted to take over the more profitable ones, not destroy them.

Today was just the warning, to make sure Benny got the message.

The rain stopped abruptly just before the LaSalle sedan entered the neighborhood, but the overcast sky threatened more to come soon, and the narrow streets were still awash. Shelly Brennan brought the car to a splashy stop half a block before reaching the speakeasy.

Beside him, Nitti opened the briefcase just enough to set the timer of the mechanism inside. Then he closed it, climbed out of the LaSalle with it, and walked the rest of the way.

He didn't worry about whether Brennan would still be there waiting when he came out. A regiment of National Guard troopers could march into the street fully armed and Brennan still wouldn't leave him in the lurch. Brennan drove for bank robbers in his spare time. He'd never been known to take off before everybody was back in the car, no matter what kind of pressure developed.

Dependable. Like Nitti.

The speakeasy had been a laundry before Benny Russo had bought it and converted it inside, three years ago. It was between a hardware store and a drugstore. The sign outside still said HAUSMAN'S LAUNDRY, but there was nobody for blocks around who didn't know what was really in there, and you didn't need any password to enter and partake: just turn the knob and walk in. The door was never locked during business hours, which was from noon to three in the morning.

Like other speakeasies high and low, in every part of town, this one operated wide open. They all did, in spite of the fact that there were some three hundred prohibition agents and three thousand police prowling Chicago, all of them sworn to uphold the law of the land, no matter how foolish this particular law might be. Which may have contributed to the amused contempt with which a lot of Chicagoans regarded both the law and its enforcers.

Some people were fond of quoting Al Capone's crack, "Hell, the cops're making more dough out've Prohibition than the bootleggers."

The only customer in the place when Frank Nitti came in was a heavy, weary-looking man in patched overalls and muddy boots, slouched at a wooden table scarred by dark cigarette burns near the bar, staring morosely into his half-empty glass of needled beer.

The bartender nodded as Nitti came over to him. "What'll you have?"

Nitti put a nickel on the bar and pointed to the tap.

While the bartender drew him a small glass of beer, Nitti set the briefcase down gently on the floor, against the bar's footrail.

As he straightened an eleven-year-old girl named Esther Blackmer came in carrying an empty beer pail. She put it up on the bar and said to the bartender, "Hello, Mr. Bartola, could you fill it up? Poppa says to tell you he'll be able to pay what he owes you this Saturday, for sure."

"Okay, sweetie, be with you in a second." The bartender placed the glass of beer in front of Nitti and took his nickel, ringing it up in the cash register. Then he picked up the pail and went to fill it from the tap. "And how's everybody at your house today, Esther?"

"They're fine, Mr. Bartola."

Nitti downed his beer quickly and strode out as the bartender asked her, "Your momma all better now?"

"Well, she still has a little cold. But she'll be all right. . . ."

The instant Nitti emerged onto the sidewalk outside, the tan LaSalle sedan shot forward from the curbside position where Brennan had been waiting with the motor running. Brennan braked to a sharp halt in front of Nitti and threw the passenger door open. Nitti jumped in beside his driver, yanked the door shut, and snapped quickly but without emotion, "*Move* it."

The sedan pulled away from the curb, accelerating as it headed off up the street. Nitti loosened his bow tie, unbuttoned his collar, and leaned back comfortably in the passenger seat, entirely relaxed.

Inside the speakeasy, the bartender put the filled beer pail on the bar in front of Esther Blackmer and said, "Here you are."

"Thank you, Mr. Bartola." She started to reach for

the pail and then noticed the briefcase against the rail near her feet. "Hey, that man forgot his bag!" She snatched it up and ran out to the sidewalk with it, looking up and down. But the man who'd left it was nowhere in sight. All she saw was a tan LaSalle driving away, almost to the cross street at the other end of the block by now.

Esther carried the briefcase back inside the speakeasy. "He's gone," she said as she walked toward the bar with it.

"That's all right, sweetie," the bartender told her. "He'll probably remember and come back for it."

At the other end of the block the LaSalle sedan was doing fifty and continuing to accelerate when it made a sharp turn into the cross street. A fruit vendor started to wheel his pushcart across the intersection at that same moment. Brennan cursed and spun the wheel to avoid it. But his tires skidded in the slippery wetness of the street. The side of the car clipped the edge of the pushcart, overturning it and spilling its contents.

"Shit!" Brennan growled, and drove away down the side street. He glanced in his rearview mirror and saw the vendor back there, standing beside his overturned cart and dumped fruit, shaking his fist after the car and cursing.

Then Brennan saw something else. "Christ! We got trouble."

Frank Nitti looked back.

A motorcycle cop was racing after them, his light flashing.

"What do I do?" Brennan whispered.

Nitti told him, coolly, "Pull over and stop."

Brennan swung to the curb. He didn't disengage the gears or turn off the motor or set the handbrake. Just pressed down on the clutch and footbrake, holding himself ready for a fast escape if it became necessary.

The cop got off his cycle and took out his summons

book as he came over to the car. "You just had an accident back there," he growled. "Don't tell me you didn't notice."

"It wasn't my fault," Brennan told him through the opened car window. "The street's slippery and—"

"But you didn't stop," the cop interrupted sharply. "That makes it hit and run. If—"

At that moment the time bomb inside the speakeasy detonated.

The explosion blasted most of the building's facade out into the street, hurling chunks of brick and wood and glass clear across the street against houses on the other side. Dark smoke billowed out after the flying debris, making it impossible to see the wreckage inside. There were no screams behind that smoke. The only sound in there came from the ceiling collapsing.

The explosion was loud enough to be heard clearly a block away, around the corner in the side street where the motorcycle cop stood beside the LaSalle sedan. The cop had no trouble identifying that sound. It wasn't the first time he'd heard a bomb go off in Chicago.

"What the hell . . ." he rasped, looking in the direction of the blast. Then he scowled at the two men in the car that had just come from that direction.

The driver, the cop thought, could be anything. But the man in the passenger seat could be only one thing: a hood. The cop had seen enough of them in his time to spot the type instantly. The man's clothes said he was a prosperous hood. His face—and especially those eyes— said he was a dangerous one.

Surreptitiously the cop lowered his right hand to the holster on his hip, unfastening the strap that held his gun securely inside it. He kept his hand close to the gun as he demanded, "Show me some identification."

Brennan gripped the steering wheel and leaned back a bit, studying the street ahead through the windshield. The motor was still running. All he'd have to do was take his feet off the clutch and brake and jam down on the gas pedal. . . .

Nitti reached under the lapel of his blue serge jacket.

The cop's right hand closed around the grip of his holstered gun.

But what Nitti drew out from inside his jacket was a large business card. He reached across Brennan and held the card out the open window. The cop took it with his left hand.

The card bore the engraved name and seal of Chicago's mayor. The cop turned it over. On the other side was written, with a neat slanting penmanship; "To whom it may concern: Please extend to the bearer, Mr. Frank Nitti, all possible courtesy and consideration. Wm. Thompson, Mayor, City of Chicago."

The cop recognized the handwriting. It was not the first time he'd seen a card like this one. He returned it and stepped back from the car, saluting.

"Sorry to bother you, sir."

"That's all right, Officer," Nitti assured him. And then to Brennan: "Let's go."

They were two blocks away when the first police cars and fire engines screamed past them, racing to the smoking wreckage of the little speakeasy where the bartender, the customer who'd been at the table, and a little girl named Esther Blackmer had just died.

None of the three was any longer recognizable.

It was shortly after ten o'clock that night that Eliot Ness first encountered a Chicago policeman named James Malone.

FOUR

The dilapidated two-story house where the informer lived was part of a row of similar houses between South Wabash and the Elevated tracks southeast of the Dearborn station. The elderly couple who owned the house occupied the top floor. The informer, an ex-con named Stash Moser, rented the ground floor. His apartment had both a front door onto the porch and street and a back door into an alley. Eliot Ness used the back when he left his informer that night.

Moser had turned off the rear-entry light before Eliot had arrived, and there were no lamps in the alley. The darkness would afford Eliot a certain measure of protection if somebody was waiting for him out there.

He didn't think there would be. He'd left his car eight blocks away, by the South Branch of the Chicago River, and made damn sure he wasn't followed from there to here. He had also reconnoitered the surrounding block for anyone watching Stash Moser's place before going in.

But in this city you could never be entirely certain the enemy wasn't around. Eliot took the .45 from under his jacket and thumbed off the safety, holding it ready when he stepped out the rear door into the dark alley. Then he put his back to the outside wall, his tall, lanky figure almost invisible against it, looking both ways and listening. There was no sound but the rumbling of a train over the nearby El tracks. None of the shadows in the alley moved.

The shorter end of the alley led directly out to the street, the longer stretch to a small lot in the interior of the block. Eliot went in that second direction, between the backs of the row houses and the high wooden fence of a scrap yard. The lot was littered with thrown-out junk that even the scrap yard didn't want. He threaded his way through it and took another alley that brought him out the other side of the block.

After checking the street outside, Eliot thumbed the automatic back on safe and slid it out of sight under his jacket. Then he began the walk back to his car.

The day's rains had ended and the clouds were breaking up, but that wasn't bringing any warmth to the night wind. The few other pedestrians Eliot passed were all wearing buttoned topcoats. Eliot wasn't. A topcoat could interfere with getting at his gun fast if he had to. Besides, cold weather never bothered him much. That was another plus from his Scandinavian heritage, along with the strong bones.

He'd put in a long day, and he was tired. But he was also unusually tense, and he walked fast, taking long strides, trying to work it out of his system. He wanted to simmer down a bit before going home to his wife.

There was ample reason for the tension. After almost two weeks of digging and planning, Eliot was ready for his first strike at Al Capone.

Tomorrow.

There'd been other attempts to nail Capone, and all of

them had failed. Bootlegging was only the most obvious of his crimes, ranging from countless murders through extortion and a long list of others. But he'd never been arrested for a single one of them here in Chicago, and the reason was obvious.

The federal government had recently estimated that Capone was paying out some twenty milion dollars a year in graft to Chicago officials ranging from beat cops to judges.

Only an enormous income from bootlegging could enable Capone to disburse that kind of cash. Cut that income down, Washington had decided, and Capone would be unable to continue paying the powers-that-be around Chicago. If he couldn't come up with it, his government protectors would fade away from him.

And that would leave Capone unprotected—vulnerable to the law.

That was what Washington had sent Eliot Ness to Chicago to do.

With some very strong backing.

He had the United States D.A.'s office in the Chicago area ready to support each move he made.

He had Chicago's chief of police cooperating, lending Eliot some of the toughest and most trusted officers from his department for a special anti-Capone flying squad under his orders.

And he had an ace in the hole, unknown as yet to anyone else but him and the district attorney: his first inside informant.

Until four months ago Stash Moser had made most of his living via armed robberies. He'd served two long sentences in prison for it. Four months ago Moser had been caught at it a third time, red-handed. A third conviction would put him behind bars for the rest of his life.

The district attorney had offered Stash Moser a behind-the-scenes deal. By the time Eliot Ness arrived in Chicago, Moser was working for the Capone organization—a very low-level employee, it was true, but in exactly the sort of place where Eliot most needed informers for his opening attack: Stash Moser was a loader in one of Capone's secret warehouses.

Two days ago he'd come up with the tip Eliot had been waiting for. The warehouse was expecting a large shipment of top-grade imported liquor from a Canadian supplier. A detachment of heavily armed Capone torpedoes had driven north to take over the truck convoy somewhere along the border.

Tonight Moser had confirmed it: the shipment had arrived. From his description of the quantity and quality of the goods, Eliot calculated what was now stored in that warehouse to be worth in excess of one million dollars.

Ripping a milion bucks out of Al Capone's pocket wouldn't ruin him. But it would inconvenience him, considerably.

It would become more than just an inconvenience if it happened again—and again. Which was precisely the strategy that had brought Eliot to Chicago: to locate, attack, and loot one after another of Capone's warehouses, liquor convoys, and breweries. If he could keep that up, Capone would soon find himself running short of enough surplus cash to cover all the local government payoffs that enabled him to operate. And when that happened, Capone would really hurt.

Tomorrow, Eliot told himself with a tight, almost vicious smile of anticipation. *Tomorrow's when the hurting begins*.

His car was parked at the east end of the road bridge spanning the river. It was a black Pontiac coupe, and it was much like each of the three suits he owned—showing its age but not yet quite shabby; still sturdy and serviceable enough. He didn't get into it immediately. There were a few details about tomorrow he hadn't worked out fully, and the cold air helped him think. Extracting a cigarette pack from his pocket, he saw with some surprise that there was only one left in it. He'd smoked a lot with Stash Moser. Sticking the last cigarette in a corner of his long mouth, Eliot crumpled the empty pack in his fist and tossed it away into the river.

From behind him a hard voice growled, "What the *hell* you think you're doing?"

Turning, Eliot found himself looking at a uniformed cop in his forties, with a tough face as Irish as his voice. In the light of the street lamp at the end of the bridge the narrowed eyes fastened on Eliot's face looked blue— and as bitter-mean as any that Eliot had ever encountered. The cop was a big man, as tall as Eliot and a good deal wider. Some of that might have been middle-age spread, but not much. Most of him still looked to be solid bone and thick muscle.

The nightstick looked like a toy imitation in his powerful hand as he pointed it at the river below. "You want to throw your garbage away, next time go find a goddamn trash basket to throw it in."

"Sorry, Officer, I didn't think."

"Well you better start practicing it. Thinking. That's what your head's intended to do, in case nobody ever told you."

Eliot experienced a spasm of annoyance—as much at the cop interrupting his thoughts as at his harsh tone. "Don't the police have more important things to do than hunting for people who drop an empty cigarette pack?"

"Yeah, but I don't happen to be doing any of them right now. We *understand* each other?"

Eliot shrugged, nodded, and started to light his cigarette.

The cop, suddenly very alert, jabbed the end of his stick against Eliot's midsection, forcing him back against the Pontiac and holding him there at arm's length. "Okay, pal," he said in a softer but more menacing voice, "why're you packin'?"

Eliot stared at him, momentarily not understanding what the cop was saying.

The cop continued to hold him pinned by the night-stick. "Why are you wearing a gun?"

Eliot relaxed a bit. "I have a permit. I'm an agent with the Treasury Department."

"Oh." The cop studied Eliot, then lowered his night-stick. "All right. But you remember what I told you, about throwing your trash around." His voice was still tough but had lost the unpleasant abrasive edge. He turned and strolled off toward the bridge.

Eliot stared after him, then flicked his cigarette into the river and stode after him.

"Wait a second, wait a second! What the hell kind of police do you *have* in this goddamned city? What do they teach you? You just turned your back on an armed man!"

The cop stopped and looked at him. "You've got a right to pack a gun. You're a Treasury officer."

"How do you know that? I just *told* you that. I could be lying."

"Now *who*," the cop demanded with a certain amount of dry scorn, "would go around claiming to be one of *those*, if he wasn't?"

Eliot felt his face get hot. The implication was clear, and this wasn't the first time he'd come across it. There were a lot of federal agents in Chicago— and so far they didn't seem to be having much success in enforcing the law. People wondered why, and drew certain odious conclusions. More odious because they were not entirely untrue, obviously.

"What's that supposed to mean?" he demanded angrily.

The cop shrugged. "Whatever you care to make of it, I suppose."

"Not every agent is on the take," Eliot snapped, furious.

"If you say so."

"No more than every *cop* is on the take!"

"If you say so," the cop repeated, in the same tone. But he was regarding Eliot with a slightly different expression now. Somewhat the way Eliot usually looked at people. With eyes that measured what they saw. He added mildly, "But I'm a lot older than you, fella, which means I've been around a good bit longer. And I'll tell you one sad fact I've noticed: an honest man's getting harder to find than people who're careful where they toss their garbage."

"What's your name and unit?" Eliot demanded.

The cop indicated his insignia. "The unit's right here, and the name's James Malone. Why? You got a beef? You wanta report me for disrespect?"

Eliot drew a slow breath, calming himself down. "No, I'm sorry if I sounded that way. Maybe I'm a little too edgy tonight." He paused, studying Malone. "Tell me something. How did you know I had a gun? I thought it doesn't show."

"Whaddya want, a free lesson in police work?" Malone's smile surprised Eliot. "You okay, pal?"

"Yeah—I just, it's been a long day. I guess I'm feeling tired."

"You going home now?"

Eliot nodded. "I was about to."

"Well, then you just fulfilled the first rule of law enforcement: make sure when your shift is over you go home—alive." He smiled that surprising smile again. "Here endeth the lesson."

With that, James Malone turned away. As he did so he took from his pocket a small chain with a key on one end and an old medallion on the other. Twirling the medallion, he headed onto the bridge.

Eliot Ness remained where he was for a while, thoughtfully watching Malone go off across it.

FIVE

The small frame house Eliot Ness had rented was in a modest residential neighborhood near the University of Chicago. He and Catherine had chosen this one because it was also only three blocks from the elementary school where they had enrolled their daughter, Cora. Catherine was walking Cora to school, early the next morning, when Eliot picked up the paper the newsboy had tossed on their porch, curious to see if there was anything of interest in it.

He started to turn back into the house as he glanced at the front page. Then he stopped, staring at the headline and picture.

The headline read "CHILD SLAIN AS BOOZE WAR EXPLODES AGAIN."

The picture was of Esther Blackmer, the girl who had been killed yesterday in the speakeasy bombing. It was a snapshot that had been taken a few months ago, on her eleventh birthday—the last she would ever have.

Something very cold crept into Eliot's eyes as he read

the accompanying news report. The last paragraph said the police had so far been unable to turn up a single lead to who might have planted the bomb.

Eliot looked again at the dead girl's smile. Then he tucked the paper under his arm and went back into the kitchen where he'd just had breakfast with Catherine— and his own little girl. Pouring himself a second cup of coffee, he carried it and the paper to the little room he had fixed up as a home office for himself.

His jacket hung on the back of the chair facing the opened rolltop desk. On the desk were the map and the sketch he'd spent some time studying last night before going to sleep.

The sketch was the one he'd made from Stash Moser's detailed description of the warehouse. He'd marked the positions of its truck entrance, the door beside it, the door in the rear, and a trap door in the roof. There were no windows that could be used to get in or out of.

The map was of the section of the city around the warehouse. On it Eliot had noted the best approaches for his raiding force, plus the positions to be taken by members of a backup force to trap any Capone gorillas that tried to escape during the attack. According to Moser there were always at least five of those on guard inside the place, day and night, heavily armed. Eliot intended to nab every one of them red-handed, right there with their weapons and illicit liquor.

He put the coffee and newspaper down on the small table beside his chair. For several seconds he continued to stand there, unable to tear his eyes away from the picture of Esther Blackmer. Finally he sat down, took a drink of coffee, and gave the map some further study. He marked another point where it would be wise to station some of his backup team and was having another sip of coffee when his phone rang.

The call was from Mike Casey, deputy to the Chicago

police chief. The one assigned by the chief to act as liaison between himself and Eliot and the newly formed flying squad.

Deputy Chief Mike Casey had risen through the ranks on sheer ability, with no help from any higher-up connections. He was an intelligent, pragmatic officer with a load of easygoing Irish charm and a wealth of street-level experience. Casey had been giving Eliot the benefit of that experience unstintingly, though he had also given his honest opinion that the odds were very much against Eliot achieving much.

Too many others had tried to nail Capone, Casey pointed out, and no matter what method they'd used, Capone had continued to walk free and smiling, unscathed.

"Sorry to bother you at home this early, Eliot," Casey said.

"That's all right, Mike. What's up?"

"I just got a call from the chief. He's setting up a conference at headquarters at noon between you and a few members of the local press. They been hearing about you and bugging him. The chief decided it's time you satisfy their curiosity a little."

"*What* have they been hearing about me?" Eliot asked tightly.

"Relax, nothing specific. Just that you've come here from Washington to try puttin' a crimp in the bootleg racket."

"I must have a press agent I don't know about."

Mike Casey chuckled. "Probably the chief himself. He'll be at your press conference, too—just to let everybody know he's solidly behind you. In case you make any sudden move that happens to turn out interesting."

"As a matter of fact," Eliot told him, "I have a feeling I'm about to. Though not anything I'd want those reporters to get wind of ahead of time."

"Don't worry, all they'll be expecting from you is

what they're used to. Some pithy remarks in a determined tone, adding up to absolutely nothing new."

"Mike, I've got to see the U.S. district attorney this morning before I come in to headquarters. Could you speak to Lieutenant Alderson for me before then? I'd like him to gather together every member of that flying squad for a meeting with me in the ready room immediately after lunch."

"Sure. Guess it's my turn to ask what's up."

"I learned the location of a warehouse last night. Loaded. We're going to raid it."

"Beautiful. When?"

"Tonight. There're too many people wandering around that area in the daytime. I don't want any innocent passersby getting hurt if we run into shooting opposition."

"Tonight—that gives you plenty of time to get it prepared."

"We'll need it—to have all the equipment and transport ready. And to make sure every man in that flying squad knows exactly what I want him to do and exactly when to do it."

"I'll give Alderson the order. *You* make sure you're on time for that meet with the press, or the chief'll be miffed. And it'll be *my* ass."

"I'll be there. With a few of those pithy statements you mentioned. I doubt it'll be anything that'll stop the press boys from snoring."

Mike Casey chuckled again as he hung up.

Eliot was staring at the newspaper again when Catherine entered the room

She was keenly attuned to her husband's moods, and what she read in his expression made her ask quickly, "What's the matter, Eliot?"

He gestured at the front page of the paper.

Catherine looked at it and nodded slowly. "Yes, I

know. I heard it on the radio last night, before you came home. I didn't think you needed to hear about it before going to bed." She was silent for a moment as she regarded the picture of the dead girl. "What kind of animals are they—men who could do a thing like that?"

"You just named it," Eliot told her. *"Animals."*

He said it without much show of emotion, but that didn't mislead her. Most people just saw his placid exterior and didn't have an inkling of what went on inside him. Catherine knew. She'd known since way back when they'd met in college.

She had been taking liberal arts. Eliot had been studying business. But when he told her, just before he proposed to her, that he'd decided he didn't want to become a businessman, she didn't have to ask him why. Because she knew the reasons.

He needed something with action and excitement that could channel those fierce energies that burned inside him. Coupled with a purpose that had meaning to him. A feeling of fighting on the side of decency—against evil. That would sound corny these days, and he knew it, and that's why he would never express it. But it was always there.

Catherine didn't say any of this to him now. What she did say, quietly, was, *"Get* those animals, Eliot. Put them away where they can't do things like this anymore."

He smiled slightly. "I'm surely going to give it my best. Starting tonight, by the way. Don't expect me home. I probably won't be back before dawn, or later."

"I also expect you won't be taking the time off to go out and get yourself a decent meal, as usual. I'll fix you something you can eat at your desk or on the run. Okay?"

"Okay," he said, and watched fondly as she went off to the kitchen.

She worked quickly, preparing two thick sandwiches and slicing some carrots. Noticing the wall calendar still showed yesterday's date, Catherine tore off that page and used it to wrap the carrots. Wrapping the sandwiches in waxed paper, she put them in a brown paper bag with the carrots and added a candy bar.

Then she hesitated, and took out the carrots. Unwrapping them, she got a pencil from the counter and wrote a short note on the calendar page. With a smile, she rewrapped the carrots in it, put them in the bag, and went back to Eliot's study. She found him getting ready to leave: putting the sketch and map into his briefcase along with a list of detailed notes he'd made for his meeting with the flying squad.

His briefcase was very much like the one Frank Nitti had left in the speakeasy the previous afternoon, though there was no way Eliot could have known that. The police team searching the wreckage hadn't found a shred of the one that had held the bomb, just as they had still not been able to turn up every part of the bodies of the three victims.

Catherine put the lunch bag inside the briefcase as her husband buttoned his vest and stood up. He opened a desk drawer and took out the shoulder rig that held his holstered .45. As he strapped it on, Catherine experienced the faint chill of fear that always jolted her when she saw him do that. The reminder that the kind of work he was going out to do could get him killed. And the nagging doubt about whether Eliot, if actually trapped into a life-or-death confrontation, would be able to use that gun to save himself.

She had once watched him take part in a competition at a police range. He'd come in second against twelve other marksmen. But putting holes in a target was not the same as shooting a man. Catherine had asked Eliot if he felt he was capable of that.

"I don't know the answer to that, honey," he'd answered after some thought. "I guess that's something nobody finds out until it happens."

He took a spare box of ammunition from the drawer and dropped it into the briefcase, closed it, and stood up. Catherine took his jacket off the back of the chair, and he let her help him put it on. Turning, he held her face between his hands and kissed her softly.

Catherine stepped back after a long moment and looked up at him with a small smile. "I love you too—but you have to go to work now, so don't get me all excited."

Slipping an arm around his waist, she walked Eliot out onto the front porch. She stayed there watching him walk down to the Pontiac coupe and get in. As he drove off she raised a hand and waved.

Then she lowered the hand and crossed her fingers.

SIX

The press conference that noon took place in a conference room at the Chicago police headquarters. There were nine reporters present, three with flash cameras. Eliot sat at the front of the room facing them, with the chief of police standing beside him making a long, rambling introductory speech to which the reporters weren't paying much attention.

Deputy Chief Mike Casey, seated in a corner at the back of the room behind the reporters, didn't seem to find his chief's words too fascinating, either. Casey was a strongly built man in his forties, with heavy sloping shoulders and the start of a solid beer belly. He sat with his thick arms crossed on his uniformed chest, a bored expression on his florid, blunt-featured face. Several times his gaze met Eliot's and he permitted himself a small, cynical smile.

Eliot stopped himself from responding with a similar smile, aware that all the reporters' eyes were studying him curiously. He listened with considerable relief as the tone of the police chief's voice indicated he was finally grinding toward the end of his speech.

The chief was saying how much he deplored—as he was sure all decent citizens deplored—the horrible speakeasy bombing incident of the previous afternoon. "I want to assure all of you," he told the reporters, "that investigators of my department are working around the clock to solve this crime and find the bootleggers responsible. I just want to remind you at this point that bootlegging and the many brutal crimes associated with it are a *nationwide* problem, not just something that happens in Chicago. I also want to point out that I and my department have over the past years done everything humanly possible, under difficult conditions, to eradicate this problem from our city."

The police chief paused for effect and then stated heavily, "And we intend to *continue* to do so." He gestured at Eliot. "And this gentleman, Mr. Eliot Ness, is the special agent of the Treasury Department who has been sent by Washington to cooperate with me and my department in our efforts." He turned to Eliot. "Would you say a few words to the gentlemen of the press, Mr. Ness?"

Eliot stood up reluctantly. It was too early to let outsiders into the methods he intended to use to carry out what he'd been sent to do. After tonight, and a few more raids like it, his tactics would become apparent to all. Then he could make public statements that got down to specifics. Until then he could only throw some meaningless generalities at these reporters, as the chief of police had just done, and that wasn't going to endear him to either the press or the public.

But the chief had given him his department's full cooperation, which obligated Eliot to cooperate in turn, courteously going along with the chief's public relations play.

"At the request of the city of Chicago," Eliot told the

reporters, "the federal government has inaugurated a special program to deal with the flow of illegal liquor and the violence which it creates."

"What's this *special* program consist of?" a reporter tossed at him, reaching immediately for the specifics Eliot wasn't yet prepared to divulge.

"I, and other agents of the federal government," he sidestepped blandly, "will be working in conjunction with the Chicago police and other enforcement bodies to enforce Prohibition under the provisions of the Volstead Act."

"Isn't this just another showpiece program?" a second reporter demanded. "Like a lot of others we've seen come and go in this city?"

Before Eliot could deal with that one there was another from a third reporter: "How do you *feel* about Prohibition, Mr. Ness? I mean you personally. As an ordinary citizen, not as a government spokesman."

Eliot responded to both questions in turn, rapidly. "It's *not* just a showpiece, and I'll tell you exactly how I feel about Prohibition. It's the law of the land. And I'm neither an ordinary citizen nor a government spokesman. I'm an officer sworn to enforce the laws of the land. And I intend to."

"Do you really think you can arrest everybody who takes a drink, Mr. Ness?"

"I'm not after people who take a drink," Eliot snapped back. "I'm after the murderous gangsters who are getting rich on bootlegging. Monsters like an Al Capone, who is able to use his enormous illicit profits to corrupt the process of law and government in this country."

"Sounds to me," drawled a questioner sardonically, "like you consider yourself to be something of a crusader, Mr. Ness. Charging on your white horse against a dragon. Is that how you see it?"

"We all know dragons don't exist," Eliot said quietly.

"Except in fairy tales and legends, right? But they're there to symbolize something. Something that *does* exist. Most of your papers carried a photograph today— of a little girl who should have had all of her life ahead of her. But she was torn apart by a bomb in a speakeasy yesterday afternoon. I suggest you look at that picture again, next time you think of Capone as a harmless mythical dragon."

That one the reporters knew to be damn good copy. Their pencils scribbled swiftly, taking down every word. But after that their questions quite understandably narrowed down on exactly how Eliot intended to carry out his mission. He fielded them as best he could without telling them anything he didn't want known yet. He couldn't get too sore at the way their queries took on an increasingly sarcastic tone. They'd heard too many spout these same general noble intentions—and the net result so far had been an Al Capone who kept getting stronger and more brazen.

The chief of police soon put an end to it. He didn't want Eliot hogging too much of the limelight. "I think that's all, boys. Mr. Ness has a lot of work to do this morning."

Flashbulbs popped as cameras snapped Eliot. The chief quickly put an arm around Eliot's shoulders to make sure he got included in some of the pictures, turning on his most sincere smile. A couple of reporters shoved forward with some last questions. Letting the chief handle these, Eliot glanced toward the rear of the room.

Deputy Chief Mike Casey had risen and moved to the glass double doors there. He signaled Eliot with a movement of his solid head.

"If you'll excuse me, gentlemen," Eliot said, "I do have my work to get on with." He disengaged himself from the police chief and moved around the reporters to the rear of the room.

A pensioner cop opened one of the double doors to let Eliot go through into the wide corridor where Mike Casey stood waiting for him.

"Nice talk you gave the boys," Casey greeted him, straight-faced. "You're almost as good at it as the chief."

"I'm still hurting," Eliot said sourly. "So don't add insult to the injury."

Casey grinned. "I'll be merciful. About the flying squad—I told Lieutenant Alderson about you wanting the meeting right after lunch. Hope he's able to get them all together by then."

"He already has. I saw Alderson for a minute before the press conference. The whole squad'll be ready for me at one." Eliot glanced at his watch. "Less than half an hour from now."

"Can you handle it without me?" Casey asked. "I got a couple other things the chief wants me to help with. He'll want to be filled in on your operation before tonight. But I can get the details later this afternoon, from you or Alderson. Okay? You don't need me at this meeting?"

"I don't need my hand held."

"Glad to hear it. The chief does sometimes. A lot, in fact."

"That's one of the penalties of becoming invaluable, Mike."

"Valuable's what I knew I was, back when I was walking a beat. But up here in the higher echelon, I'm not always so sure." Casey shook his head moodily. Then he grinned again. "Will ya listen to me gripe—poor little successful cop." He clapped a big hand on Eliot's shoulder. "Good luck to you tonight."

A reporter from the conference room, one of the three with a camera, pushed through the double doors as Mike Casey said it—and heard him.

He wasn't slow on the uptake. His narrowing eyes switched from Casey to Eliot. "Good luck with *what*?"

Casey rasped, "Get lost, Fergy."

But the reporter kept his attention fastened on Eliot. "What *are* your real plans, Mr. Ness? What is it you've got in the works for tonight?"

Eliot gave him his bland smile. "I only know what I read in the papers."

"Come on, Mr. Ness, give me a break. Lemme ride along with you, whatever it is you're gonna do. I'll give you a big play—story and pictures. Good for you and me both."

"Can't help you," Eliot told him, holding the smile.

"This guy," Casey told him dryly, "is Ferguson. With the *Tribune*. A pretty smart reporter, but sometimes a bad boy. Pushy, needs firm handling." He took a firm grip on Ferguson's elbow. "Come on and talk to the chief, Fergy—*he* likes reporters." Casey dragged Ferguson along with him, back through the double doors into the conference room.

As Catherine had anticipated, Eliot's lunch that day was a hasty one in his office on the second floor of the headquarters building. As he took the things out of the bag she had prepared for him he spotted her handwriting on the paper she'd used to wrap the carrots. He smoothed the calendar page on his desk and smiled as he read his wife's message on the back of it:

"I am very proud of you."

Under it was drawn one of the small hearts with which Catherine sometimes signed her notes to him.

Still smiling, he folded it neatly and slipped it in the side pocket of his jacket. It would make as good a souvenir as any, later, to remind him of what was going to happen tonight. The opening attack on Al Capone.

He was finishing the last bite of his lunch when Lieutenant Alderson came into his office.

Alderson had been assigned to manage the new flying squad under Eliot's direction. He was about Eliot's height and age—a lean, ramrod-straight man in an immaculate uniform, with pale hair and dead-level brown eyes. Alderson had an impressive record of arrests behind him, along with two bravery medals and a law degree he'd obtained in night school while working as a cop. It was that combination—plus an uncle who was somebody in the state legislature—that accounted for his coming up to lieutenant so young.

A bit stiff-necked, in Eliot's opinion. The kind of career man you came across more often in the military than the police. But Eliot couldn't fault him as an officer. Alderson was as efficient as hell, and held the new squad under tight discipline.

"Mr. Ness," Alderson said, "the men are all present and waiting, if you are ready to talk to them."

"I'm ready, Lieutenant." Eliot nodded at the big canvas map rolled tightly under Alderson's arm. "That the one I asked for?"

"Yes, sir."

"Then let's get started."

"After you, sir."

Eliot led the way to the ready room.

SEVEN

The windows along one side of the ready room overlooked the big parking area behind the police headquarters. Two other walls were lined with armaments, ranging from tear-gas canisters to sawed-off repeating shotguns. The fourth wall had a big blackboard and a bigger cork bulletin board, both empty at the moment.

It was a spacious room, but the members of the flying squad filled the space. There were thirty of them, seated on the benches and rows of folding chairs, each in a uniform as immaculate as Lieutenant Alderson's, complete with jodhpurs and well-shined riding boots. All of them were young enough to be in top physical condition and old enough to have some years of street-level experience under their belts.

All thirty of them came to their feet and snapped to attention when Eliot entered with the lieutenant behind him.

Alderson inspected them with those dead-level eyes for a full ten seconds. Then he snapped, "At ease."

"You can sit down," Eliot told the squad. "Relax. This is going to take some time."

When they were all seated again he walked over to a flattop desk near the wall bearing the blackboard and bulletin board. Placing his briefcase on the desk, he turned to face them.

"I've gotten word from a reliable informant," he began, "that a very large shipment of liquor from Canada has arrived at a Capone warehouse here in Chicago. According to my information there are a number of armed guards stationed there at all times. So I hope all of you have signed on because you're looking for some action. Because you're likely to get it. We're hitting the place tonight."

Eliot paused to scan the faces of the flying squad and saw nothing but eagerness. "The gorillas on guard there," he resumed, "have been in fights before. Mostly against hijackers. They know how to shoot and don't have any qualms about shooting to kill. I want them taken. Alive if possible, but use your judgment. If anybody's got to be shot taking this place, I don't want it to be any of you. Any questions so far?"

A hand was raised.

Lieutenant Alderson identified the man. "Sergeant McGough."

"Okay, Sergeant," Eliot said, "what is it."

"About taking the men inside there," McGough said. "I was on another raid about a year ago. We used axes and sledgehammers to break in. The wood doors were easy, but it turned out there were heavy steel doors behind those. Took a helluva long time to break those in. By the time we did, there wasn't anybody left inside for us to grab. They'd all slipped away through an escape tunnel."

"This warehouse has an escape tunnel, too," Eliot told him, "as well as two other possible exits. But we know where they are and where they lead, and some of you will be stationed where you can seal each of them. I'll be getting to that in due order."

He would also be getting to the matter of steel doors. According to Stash Moser there *was* one behind this warehouse's wooden truck entrance, as well as at the rear door. But Eliot had come up with an answer to that problem a week ago, and Lieutenant Alderson had implemented it. The answer was a heavy-duty Mack truck, with souped-up power and a reinforced snowplow fastened to its front. It was waiting now in a garage three blocks from headquarters.

Eliot got his sketch and map from the briefcase, spread them on the desk, and nodded to Alderson. "Lieutenant, will you put up that map you brought in with you."

Alderson used pushpins to tack the top of the big map to the top of the bulletin board, and let it unroll. It was a large-scale map of a ten-block area surrounding the warehouse, with each street, alley, and building shown.

Eliot used a crayon to mark the warehouse with an X. "This is the location of our target. Each of the three squads to which Lieutenant Alderson has assigned you men will have a separate function. We'll have Squad A handling the attack. Squad B is to cover the warehouse exits and stop anyone who tries to get away through them. Squad C takes the perimeter—to seal off the area when the attack begins and keep people out of it until it's completed. Lieutenant, let's have those squad leaders up here."

Alderson called out the names of the three squad leaders. Eliot waited until they came to the front of the room. Then he picked up a piece of chalk and copied his sketch of the warehouse on the blackboard. When he was finished he pointed out the truck entrance to the leader of Squad A. "We'll bust in through there. Lieutenant Alderson and I will go in with your attack squad."

After going over the method and timing of the attack,

Eliot moved on to the job of Squad B, whose leader was
Sergeant McGough. "There are three possible ways to
get out of this warehouse. Split your squad into three
units to cover them." Eliot pointed out the rear door on
the blackboard. "One-third outside there. Your second
unit will need a ladder. There's a trapdoor exit in the
roof. Make sure they get to their position up there
quietly."

Eliot turned to the map. "The escape tunnel from the
warehouse leads out to this alley here." He marked it on
the map. "So the rest of your men stand guard there. I
want your three units to move in to their stations exactly
one minute before Squad A hits the front of the warehouse. Not a second before. And definitely no later. Understood?"

"Yes, sir. Exactly one minute."

Next Eliot went over the map with Lieutenant Alderson and the Squad C leader, deciding on the best places
to station each of the perimeter men and vehicles to seal
off the area during the attack. When that was settled,
Eliot went back to the blackboard and marked the area
where the armed warehouse guards usually hung out, according to Stash Moser: in front, just inside the truck
entrance.

"There are also a lot of the newly arrived cases of
liquor still piled in that front area, with a red pine-tree
emblem marked on each case. But there'll be a couple of
workmen tonight loading the cases on carts and moving
them to rear sections of the warehouse."

That brought Eliot to the problem of Stash Moser.

"I've got a man of my own in there. He's one of those
two workmen. Neither of those two is armed. *My* man
will be wearing a red bandanna around his neck. I don't
want him hurt in the attack."

"Red bandanna," Lieutenant Alderson repeated
loudly to the members of the flying squad. "Everybody
got that?" There were nods, and the lieutenant turned

back to Eliot. "Don't worry, we'll take care of your man."

"Don't take care of him too obviously. Just make sure he's not shot or roughed up. I *do* want him arrested, along with the rest of the men we catch in there."

The fact that neither Moser nor the other loader would be caught carrying a gun would be the excuse, later, for releasing them both from custody—without making anyone suspicious about it. That way Stash Moser would be able to go back to work for Eliot in some other part of the Capone organization.

It was shortly after nightfall when Eliot came out of the headquarters building into its rear parking lot. He walked to the unmarked Packard sedan the police department had assigned to him and got in the front seat beside his driver, Patrolman Preseuski, a burly young member of the flying squad, dressed for tonight's job in ordinary civilian clothes.

Eliot shut his door, settled back in his seat, and said quietly, "How we doing, Preseuski?"

His driver nodded. "They're almost ready, sir." His voice was low and tense.

Looking through the windshield, Eliot saw the members of his B and C squads climbing into their cars. The ten-man A Squad stood waiting for their own vehicle to arrive. Each of them carried either a carbine or a shotgun.

"Nervous?" Eliot asked Preseuski.

"No, sir. A little excited. But not scared, if that's what you mean."

"*Be* a little scared," Eliot told him. "Helps a man react faster in a tight situation."

He reached into his pocket for his cigarettes. His hand came out holding something else as well. He looked and saw it was the folded note from Catherine. Lighting a cigarette, he returned the pack and the note to his pocket. "You married, Preseuski?"

"Yes, sir. Few years now."

"It's nice, having the right kind of woman on your side."

"That's what I always said, sir. The right kind. They're not that easy to find."

At that moment the big Mack truck came into view, turning out of the dark street into the parking lot. The reinforced snowplow jutting from the front of it made the truck look like some kind of prehistoric monster as it came through the shadows.

Lieutenant Alderson was up in its cab with the driver. The truck slowed to a halt. Squad A moved around to the back of it and started climbing inside.

Eliot looked at his watch. There were still sixteen minutes left before the units of the flying squad were due to start out for the warehouse area. But he wanted to be there, looking the place over, before the rest arrived.

He flicked his cigarette out the window. "Let's go, Preseuski."

EIGHT

It was a manufacturing and industrial storage area, its air laden with acrid dust and the fumes of a nearby chemical plant. The streets were murky and empty of life now, the jigsaw puzzle of factories, warehouses, and fenced truck-parking lots locked up tight for the night.

The car in which Eliot and his driver sat was parked in a pool of darkness against the side wall of a cardboard-box factory. Half a block away the only street lamp in sight shone on one corner of an intersection. A short half block past that was the liquor warehouse.

A solid, square building of sooty brick, it was supposed to be a warehouse for farm machinery spare parts. But Capone had quietly acquired it two years ago, though no official documents in any government bureau recorded the change.

It appeared as dead as everything else for blocks around. They'd driven past it slowly, and then Eliot had taken a stealthy stroll around it. No interior light showed; no sounds could be heard from inside.

Eliot held a sawed-off shotgun across his knees. Beside him Preseuski had an ax in his left hand and his revolver gripped in his right. They had only a few more minutes to wait. By now Squad C would be establishing itself around the perimeter, Squad B would be separating into three units to block the exit points, and the attack squad would be approaching in the truck with its snowplow snout.

A man appeared out of a narrow alley near the intersection. He stopped and took a long look up and down the street, seeming to search for something. The shadows where he stood were too thick for Eliot to make out what the man looked like. He seemed to be carrying something bulky but not too large in one hand.

The man moved suddenly, walking swiftly to the intersection. That brought him closer to the car, but it was doubtful if he could see it in the pool of darkness and certain he could not see the two men in it. When he reached the intersection he stopped again, taking a long look up each of the streets that led to it.

When the street lamp shone on him Eliot saw what it was he was carrying and realized who he was. With a soft, vicious curse, Eliot got out of the car and headed for him as fast as he could without being too noisy about it.

The man heard him in the last second and twisted to face him, then grinned when he recognized him.

Eliot kept his voice low, through clenched teeth. "You son of a bitch! How'd you find out?"

"Elementary," Ferguson told him, delighted with himself. "Once I realized something was up for tonight. I know an awful lot of cops—including a few that got attached to that flying squad of yours. Oh, don't worry, none of them told me anything. I just hung around headquarters and kept an eye on them. And followed when they headed this way. Some of your force began setting up roadblocks near here, so I left my car and slipped in through an alley, hunting for the action point. Looks like I've found it, eh?"

"Get out of here, fast," Eliot snapped. "Before I smash both your face and your camera."

"Be *reasonable*," the reporter-photographer pleaded. "My being along can be good news for you. I get a camera-witness scoop and you get a big splash on the front page that'll get all the support you need for what you're trying to do. Come on, Mr. Ness."

Preseuski, coming up beside Eliot, said, "I can handcuff him to the wheel. Or knock him cold and . . ."

But it was too late by then to do anything much about Ferguson's presence. The Mack truck with the snowplow turned a corner two blocks away and came rolling toward the liquor warehouse.

"Stay back out of the way or what you're likely to get is shot." Eliot sprinted to meet the fast-approaching truck, with Preseuski close behind him.

The truck was almost to the warehouse when it abruptly slowed down. Lieutenant Alderson and the attack squad jumped from it with their weapons held at the ready. Half the men joined Alderson on one side of the truck while the remaining half swung to the other side of it with their squad leader. Eliot came up alongside the squad leader as the Mack truck surged forward under full power.

Its snowplow splintered the wood door of the warehouse truck entrance—and clanged against the steel inner door. For two seconds the engine roared and the tires spun, shrieking and smoking. The metal barrier buckled and then ripped out of its hinges, falling inward with a deafening crash.

The truck rolled over it and bucked to a halt inside the warehouse.

Two men in overalls had been playing poker at a fold-

ing table. The cards had fallen from their hands as the
snowplow smashed through at them. Staring open-
mouthed at its bent prow looming over them, they
started to raise their hands. The hands jerked up full-
stretch above their heads when the men and guns of the
attack force came charging in around both sides of the
truck.

Eliot and his shotgun reached them first. "Federal officers," he informed the two cardplayers flatly, "and
you're under arrest for violations of the Volstead Act."

They sat frozen as the attack squad flowed past them,
led by Lieutenant Alderson and the squad leader, and
fanned out to search the warehouse for more of its
guards. Only one squad member remained behind with
Eliot and Preseuski, covering the pair at the card table.

There were five crates near the table. The red pine
tree stamped on each brought a grin to Eliot's face. He
shifted the shotgun to his left hand and held out his right.
Preseuski handed him the ax. Eliot smashed the top of
the nearest crate open with it. As he put down the ax he
spotted Ferguson edging in beside the truck with his
camera.

"Well," Eliot told him, "if you want to take a picture,
now's the time to take it." He reached into the broken
case, brushing aside the packing excelsior.

He began to frown as his hand failed to touch anything but more packing. Puzzled, he dug deeper. His
fingers closed around something solid. But it didn't feel
like a bottle. Disengaging it from the concealing excelsior, he saw what it was: a gaily colored Japanese parasol.

As he pulled it all the way out of the crate it popped
open.

A flashbulb flared as Ferguson snapped his picture of
Eliot staring dumbfounded at the open parasol in his
hand.

"Get him out of here!" Eliot snarled. "I mean *now*!"

Preseuski grabbed Ferguson and half threw him out toward the street, following threateningly to make sure he kept going.

Eliot looked around him at the other pine-tree crates. There was a hard knot forming in the pit of his stomach. He didn't pick up the ax again. Instead he turned and began frisking the two men at the card table.

Neither was armed. At that point that didn't surprise Eliot.

By then Lieutenant Alderson had reached the rear door of the warehouse and unlocked it, letting in the members of B Squad stationed out back. Some of the flying squad began working their way back toward Eliot, methodically smashing open every crate they came upon. The rest of the men climbed to the second floor and spread out to search there.

They failed to turn up a single bottle of liquor.

They didn't find any weapons, either.

Nor did they find any other men in the warehouse other than the pair of cardplayers. That hit Eliot hardest when they brought him the news.

Stash Moser wasn't there.

When the Packard turned into the street of frame row houses near the El tracks Eliot jumped out before Preseuski could bring it to a full stop at the curb.

He didn't bother with any stealthy approach this time. Yanking the automatic from his shoulder holster, he charged straight across the sidewalk to the front door of Stash Moser's ground-floor apartment.

The door was ajar. There was a light on inside. Eliot kicked the door all the way open and dodged in.

He didn't have to go far. Stash Moser was in the front room.

The red bandanna wasn't around his neck. It was

wadded deep inside his strained-open mouth. It looked like he'd swallowed most of it.

Stash Moser's arms were spread wide. The handles of the ice picks that pinned his hands to the floor protruded from his palms.

The third ice pick handle protruded from his heart.

"Christ!" Preseuski whispered when he came in behind Eliot and saw what was on the floor.

"There's a phone in the next room," Eliot told him tonelessly. "Call Homicide and stay put till they get a team here."

Preseuski went into the next room. Eliot stood for several moments longer staring down at his murdered informer. Then he turned away and walked back outside.

He stopped when he reached the sidewalk, taking deep breaths of the cold night air. Reaching automatically into his pocket for his cigarettes, his fingers touched the folded square of paper there. He brought it out and held it in his palm, remembering what Catherine had written on it: *I am very proud of you.*

Eliot crushed it in his fist and started to throw it away from him. But that reminded him of James Malone, the mean-eyed cop who'd bawled him out the previous night by the bridge. He continued to think about Malone for a bit.

Then he stuck his wife's crumpled note back in his pocket. It would still serve as a souvenir, he told himself bitterly. A reminder that he had been far too sure of himself—and had badly underestimated the cunning of the enemy.

He would have to do some very hard thinking about what had gone wrong tonight, and why it had gone wrong, before attempting any further moves against that enemy.

He walked as he thought. Walked for hours. Aimlessly, it seemed. If there was any direction in his night walk through the city, he was not consciously aware of it.

An hour before midnight, Eliot suddenly realized that he had just turned into Michigan Avenue south of the Loop and was walking toward the Lexington Hotel—Al Capone's headquarters.

NINE

The Lexington was an old-fashioned, ten-story hotel with turrets and banks of bay windows. It had been constructed in the 1890s to accommodate some of the inflow of visitors to the Chicago World's Fair. Al Capone had taken it over in 1928. He liked its central location, solid walls, and spacious high-ceilinged rooms.

The most luxurious of these rooms were the six that comprised Capone's personal living suite, on the fourth floor. It was as secure as it was opulent. All the other rooms on that floor were taken by his closest lieutenants, and the corridors were patrolled by hoods toting pistols and tommy guns. An interloper would have found it virtually impossible to get even as far as that floor. The ones below and above it were also inhabited exclusively by members of the Capone gang, including such auxiliaries as girlfriends and Capone's own ever-changing stable of mistresses.

Capone had another headquarters, equally comfortable and fortresslike, though not so central. It was the three-story Hawthorne Hotel, just across the city line in Cicero. He had established himself out there during a period when Chicago had experienced a short-lived reform administration that had sometimes made his presence in the city irksome.

In taking over the Hawthorne, Capone had gone on to take over the rest of Cicero. It became known as a place where anything went—with one exception. Its citizens could tolerate Capone killings, extortions, speakeasies, gambling, and other assorted rackets; but, being intensely moral, they balked at prostitution. Capone graciously conceded: no conspicuous whoring in Cicero. He grabbed control of a few little suburban communities on the edges of Cicero and put his brothels in there.

Capone liked Cicero and the Hawthorne fine. But nowadays he was more likely to be found back in the Lexington. He had nothing to fear from Chicago's present administration. Chicago was *his*: that point had been hammered home once and for all two years ago.

That had been when a citizens crime commission had tried to think up some way to prevent a repetition of the violence of the previous election, with voters and election officials opposed to Capone candidates threatened and beaten in the streets of Chicago. There was only one way to stop that kind of thing, they'd finally decided. The head of the commission—a highly respected seventy-five-year-old patrician—had gone to the Lexington Hotel to ask Al Capone to please do something about it. Flattered, Capone said he would—and did. The next election was a peaceful one.

But at a price: the spectacle of the dignified old aristocrat humbling himself before a twenty-nine-year-old gangster.

After that people began calling the Lexington Hotel "Capone's Castle."

Across the street from it, Eliot Ness stood against a wall with his fists stuffed in his pockets, gazing up bitterly at the lights showing inside the fourth floor's big bay windows.

Eliot asked himself what he was doing there. Hoping to bring the dragon's lair crashing down by hurling his hatred at it? Trying to focus his attention on his enemy at close range in order to read his mind? He told himself he was a fool. He wasn't some kind of witch doctor, and his enemy couldn't be defeated by any occult mental powers. He knew he should go home, get a solid night's sleep, and rethink his methods with a clear head after he shook off his fatigue and depression.

Yet he continued to stand there for some time, looking across Michigan Avenue at the Lexington. Wondering if Capone was in there now, gloating over the ease with which he'd beaten the United States government once again—this time in the person of Eliot Ness.

Capone *was* in there at that moment—but not thinking about Eliot Ness. The new federal agent in town was no more to Capone that a flea he had already swatted and could forget. He had much more important things on his mind at the moment.

He was attending to them with his bookkeeper, a fifty-year-old man named Walter Payne, in the sumptuous office next to his bedroom suite. They were going over the economic ramifications of Capone's latest acquisitions in the world of legitimate business and industry.

Keeping the boss current on matters like these required Payne to consult the small ledgers he'd spread out on the huge, ebony-topped desk. There were more little ledgers in the briefcase with a combination lock that he always carried with him. It was in these ledgers that Walter Payne kept his daily records of Capone's incredibly diverse and convoluted financial involvements.

Whenever he could find the time, Payne would transfer these daily records to much larger ledgers that were kept in his office safe down the hall from Capone's rooms on the fourth floor, and then tear those pages out of the portable ledgers and burn them. But he was always falling behind in that task. Al Capone's business affairs kept multiplying so fast, constantly changing. Keeping track of the details of that much income and outflow was a staggering job.

The most difficult aspect, of course, was the numerous list of bribes to be paid out. There were so very many, ranging from five dollars each week to clerks in various government bureaus, to several thousands per month to higher functionaries and judges, to the occasional hundred-thousand or million-dollar one-time "bonus" at the very top. And Payne had to supervise it all.

Yet Walter Payne did manage to keep on top of it all—through unstinting hard work and the exercise of an exceptional one-talent mind, for which Capone showed his appreciation with both considerable monetary rewards and unflagging respect.

It was a strange association. No two men could have been more different than Walter Payne and the hulking, physically powerful Capone. Payne was small and skinny, his narrow shoulders permanently bowed. He wore a thick mustache to compensate for a weak chin, had sparse white hair, and his nearsighted eyes seemed to be drowning behind the thick lenses of his glasses.

The differences extended to more than physique. Payne had a horror of physical violence and had never been in a fistfight even as a boy. Nor had he ever used or carried a weapon—which made him resent deeply when some journalists referred to him as a gangster. He was not: he was a bookkeeper.

And as such, Payne had known Capone as long as any man in the organization, from the very start of Capone's climb to the top. Payne had been the bookkeeper for Big Jim Colosimo's cafe when Big Jim's lieutenant, Johnny

Torrio, had first brought young Al Capone to Chicago as an enforcer. When Torrio had taken over after Big Jim's demise, he'd begun organizing the rackets along more efficient lines. He'd understood that a growing organization needed strict financial supervision—and had given that job to Walter Payne.

Torrio had conveyed his organizational understanding and respect for Payne's talents to Capone before quitting the business after almost getting killed in a shooting attack. Capone had been the boss, and Payne his bookkeeper, ever since.

Capone trusted him as he did few others. It was Payne who carried huge amounts of Capone cash out of the country to deal with foreign liquor suppliers, for example. That was not only because Capone could trust him. Prohibition existed only in the United States. In all other parts of the world large-scale liquor dealers were respectable citizens. They didn't like dealing with obvious criminal types. Walter Payne was someone they felt comfortable with.

There was one other facet to this close relationship between gangster and bookkeeper: Capone had become genuinely fond of Payne over the years. Payne was flattered by the affection. But there were times when its intensity terrified him.

Like the time a tough bootlegger, Nick Ryan, had slapped Payne around in a restaurant just because he was drunk and found the puny bookkeeper's timidity contemptible. Capone had taken one look at Payne's split lip and black eye and had gone hunting Ryan. He'd found him and shot him five times in the head, at a distance of two inches, spattering himself with pieces of Ryan's skull and brains.

There had been plenty of witnesses to that. Capone had vanished for a few days. By the time he'd reappeared one witness had been found in the Chicago River, another had disappeared, and the rest had changed their minds about what they'd seen.

Walter Payne shuddered with horror whenever he remembered that incident. Sometimes he had nightmares about it.

But Capone could show his affection in small, touching ways, too. As he did now, on noticing that Payne's coffee cup was empty. Capone growled at Tony Accardo, the bodyguard slouched in an easy chair near the office door, "Tony, get Mr. Payne a fresh cup of coffee."

Payne was the only one Capone called "Mister." Another sign of his respect.

When Accardo returned with the coffee, Payne thanked him. Capone just grunted and went on questioning Payne about the latest figures in his daily record books. Tony Accardo wandered over to the bay window and stood there, gazing out absently as he lit himself a cigar.

Then he tensed a bit, spotting the tall, lanky figure standing across the street looking up at the hotel.

Accardo watched him for a couple of minutes. The figure didn't move. "Boss," Accardo said, "there's a guy out there watching the place. I think he's lookin' up here."

"Anybody we know?"

"Can't make out his face." Accardo smiled a little. "Maybe a tourist? Wants to come in and ask for your autograph but he's shy?"

Capone laughed. He enjoyed being a celebrity. Then he stopped laughing. People did sometimes hang around outside hoping for a glimpse of him, like they did outside the houses of Hollywood movie stars. But not at night.

"Get a few of the boys," he told Accardo, "and go down and check him out."

Accardo went out into the corridor and looked over the guards on duty along it. At that moment Frank Nitti emerged from his room with a girl. Accardo walked over, told the girl to get lost, and explained to Nitti what was up. The two of them went downstairs together.

Whatever the guy watching the hotel was, Accardo didn't figure he needed more than one man along to handle him. Not when that one was the Enforcer.

But when they got outside, the tall lanky figure Accardo had seen was no longer there.

Nitti and Accardo circled for a few blocks around, searching, but the guy had disappeared, whoever he was.

TEN

The newspaper that landed on the front porch the next morning had the liquor raid fiasco spread across the front page.

There was the picture Ferguson had snapped of Eliot standing beside the crate he'd just broken open, with the Japanese parasol in his hand and a stunned look on his face, the snowplow protruding through the smashed warehouse door behind him.

Next to the photo was a cartoon of Eliot dressed as a knight astride a snowplow, intent on skewering Al Capone with his lance. Capone was depicted holding a glass of beer, leaning back on his throne and laughing as he watched the federal Prohibition agent ride blindly past him.

The caption read: 'Crusader Fed Busts Out."

Eliot carried the paper down to his Pontiac and drove off without waiting for Catherine to return from walking Cora to school.

When he reached his office at headquarters the secretary assigned to him, a police clerk named Ben Ruggles, had a message for him. "Mr. Ness, Deputy Chief Casey asked to see you in his office, soon's you came in."

"I'll bet," Eliot said tightly. He took the elevator up to the top floor and strode down the hallway, past Casey's secretary and into his office.

Mike Casey was seated behind his desk, speaking with Lieutenant Alderson, who stood stiffly before him. Their conversation came to an abrupt stop when Eliot entered. The newspaper with Eliot's fiasco on the front page was on Casey's desk. Casey grabbed it hastily and dumped it into his wastebasket.

"Never mind," Eliot told him, "I've already seen it."

"That bastard Ferguson," Casey growled. "I'm gonna do my best to get him barred from headquarters for what he did."

Eliot shrugged. "Why? All he did was report what happened. None of what he wrote's a lie, and his photograph's not a fake. For that matter, that cartoon's pretty accurate, too. I don't have to like it, but it does make its point. I went after Capone, and I missed. And I guess he *is* laughing at how he tricked me into missing that badly. He's got reason to."

Casey was looking at him with embarrassed sympathy. "The chief had me in his office fifteen minutes ago, Eliot. He's pretty upset about how bad this makes all of us look. Him, especially, after that glowing speech he gave the press yesterday. He wants to know how that operation could have turned out that sour. What could I tell him? *I* don't know, and I said I'm sure you don't either."

Lieutenant Alderson said thickly, "It seems obvious to *me*." He looked from the deputy chief to Eliot. "There was a leak in our operation."

Eliot nodded but said nothing.

Casey said unhappily, "Yeah. Obvious. Trouble is, you got thirty men in that flying squad. No way to know which one of them might be a Capone spy."

The lieutenant stiffened a bit more, his face expressionless. "I hate to think it's any of *them*, sir. They're all good men."

"The spy doesn't have to be in the flying squad," Eliot pointed out. "Cops gossip between themselves, trust each other, and tell each other what they're doing. Some of the squad probably talked to their cop friends around here. Anyone they talked to could be the Capone spy."

"Could be," Casey acknowledged. "We'll have an investigation, naturally, but I don't hold out much hope for it. There's just too many people around headquarters to dig out which one loused us up."

"Too many," Eliot agreed. But he seemed to say it to himself more than to Casey, and as though the words had a different meaning for him than for the deputy police chief.

"Lieutenant," Casey said to Alderson, "would you leave us alone now."

"Yes, sir." Lieutenant Alderson gave Eliot a fellow-sufferer look as he passed him on his way out.

As Alderson shut the door behind him Eliot wandered across Casey's office, coming to a halt when he reached the windows. They overlooked the drive-in courtyard of the headquarters building. Eliot saw the police chief's chauffeured limousine down there in the courtyard, its driver waiting beside it.

Behind Eliot, Mike Casey said reluctantly, "I got to tell you something. The way the chief sees it, you're the focus of all this bad publicity we just got. He wouldn't mind if you was to quit now and go back to Washington."

"He figures that would take the heat off his police department," Eliot said flatly without turning to look at Casey. "Make it look like this mess was my fault alone."

"Yeah," Casey admitted, "that's how he figured it."

Down in the courtyard, the driver opened a rear door of the limousine as the chief of police came out of the building. The chief climbed in. His driver shut the door and got in the front seat. Eliot watched the limousine move out through the wide drive-in passage.

"Your chief," Eliot said dryly, "doesn't seem anxious to discuss it with me in person."

"You know how he is. Doesn't like unpleasant confrontations. That's why *I* get so much of his dirty work. But in this case, the one he tried to pass the buck to was the U.S. district attorney, Ralph Morgan."

Eliot turned from the windows. "How'd the D.A. take the suggestion I quit?"

"Turned it down. Pretty hard, I guess, because the chief backed off real quick, dropped the idea like he never had it. So you've still got the job. And the police department's going to continue giving you our 'full cooperation,' like they say."

"After a little behind-the-scenes failure of nerve."

"I wouldn't want you letting the chief know I told you about that, Eliot."

"You know I won't."

"Yeah." Mike Casey heaved a dramatic sigh and leaned back in his swivel chair. "Now that's off my chest, sit down and let's get to work. We got to come up with some new way to hit Capone. And maybe reorganize that flying squad while we're at it."

But Eliot was walking across his office to the door.

Startled, Casey asked, "Where are you going?"

"Out. I probably won't be around much for a couple of days. I need some thinking time. Alone."

Before Casey could say anything to that, Eliot left the office and headed for the elevator. He took it down to the ground floor. When he got off there, he stopped and looked at what somebody had pinned to a police bulletin board across from the elevator.

It was the "crusader" caricature of him from the front page of that morning's paper.

At the bottom somebody had scrawled: *The Cavalry Has Arrived!*

Eliot wasn't surprised to see that there were Chicago cops who got a kick out of his failure. Local cops everywhere resented outside law enforcement agents coming in to deal with *their* city's problems. It strongly implied that they weren't doing a good job of handling things themselves and needed the outside help. It also held a danger that the outsider would air some of their police department's dirty linen in public.

So the cartoon being on the police bulletin board was understandable. But that didn't alleviate the uneasy feeling that had already been growing before he saw it there.

He walked away from the headquarters building with that feeling growing stronger: that he was very much on his own in this war with Capone.

Al Capone didn't get to see the morning paper until after two o'clock that afternoon.

He was a late sleeper because he seldom got to bed until dawn. Nights were when he most liked to work and play.

The two girls who'd shared his bed had slipped out while Capone still slept and returned to their room upstairs. That was the way he preferred it. He liked going to bed with whores but not waking up with them.

Capone rang for his butler before climbing out of the big bed. Feeling groggy and hung over, he put the black-and-gold satin robe on over his green-and-red silk pajamas. Then he stuck his feet into the mink-lined slippers and shuffled into the bathroom.

When he came out he saw that the butler had come and gone, leaving the breakfast tray on the table. A humidor of fresh cigars had been placed to one side of the tray, the folded morning paper to the other. Capone plumped himself down and drank half a cup of coffee first. Then he shoveled in some of the eggs and bacon, with three slices of buttered toast. After downing more coffee, he opened the newspaper.

Capone's hangover began to lift as he looked at the photograph and cartoon of Eliot Ness on the front page. Laughing softly, he tossed the paper on the carpet. He lit his first cigar of the day with a deep sense of well-being.

There was nothing better, for starting a day off right, than knowing you had just kicked an enemy's teeth in.

Eliot sat on a bench near the Lincoln Park shoreline, gazing across the wind-ruffled surface of Lake Michigan while he thought it out.

Before he made any future moves, or could even lay plans for them, he had to do something about the problems that had wrecked his first move. These, he realized, boiled down to two main ones.

The first was that too many people had known about his plans for the raid last night. Any of them could be on the take, earning a little extra—or a lot extra—from Al Capone.

The second was that his only source of information about Capone's activities was dead. He had to find others.

Eliot remained there on that bench, considering possible methods of dealing with those two problems, for well over an hour. Then he left Lincoln Park and went to work.

Over the next two days he made some quiet inquiries, entirely on his own.

Then he went to pay a call on the cop who'd yelled at him for throwing his cigarette package in the river.

James Malone.

ELEVEN

James Malone lived at 1634 Racine. He had first rented the house when he got married. His wife had died in childbirth, together with the baby, when she was only twenty-six. Malone had no family left.

His father had been a cop, too. He'd been killed trying to arrest two armed robbers a couple of years before retirement. Malone's mother had died the year before he got married.

Malone often thought the house was too big for a lone man, that he should move into something smaller. Somehow he had never gotten around to doing so.

He was brewing a pot of tea in the kitchen, dressed in slacks and slippers, with a moth-eaten vest his wife had knitted him long ago over a plaid wool shirt, when the front doorbell rang.

There had been times in the past when Malone had failed to exercise sufficient caution, with painful results. And Chicago had become the sort of town where you never knew. Instead of taking the direct route down the hall from the kitchen to the entry, he detoured around toward it through his living room. An upright gramophone, from his parents, stood by the archway into the entry. He opened its lid and took out what was hidden inside: a shotgun with its barrel sawed off very short.

Carrying the shotgun in his right hand, with his finger on the trigger, Malone moved to one of the curtained living-room windows. With his left hand he gently opened the curtain a scant inch and peered out. When he saw the man standing outside, he drew back, put the shotgun away in the gramophone, and shut the lid on it. Then he went through the archway into the entry, unlocked his front door, and opened it.

Eliot smiled at him. "Remember me?"

"Yes, I do," Malone said, with no welcome in his eyes or tone. "What do you want, Mr. Ness?"

"You know my name."

"Your picture was in the papers. I recognized you, and read the story."

"Then you know I need help."

"You do indeed," Malone said with no give at all in his voice. "That doesn't say what you're doing here."

"Can I come in and talk a little?"

Malone studied Eliot with those mean, shrewd eyes. Then he answered by shrugging a heavy shoulder and stepping aside to let Eliot come in. He closed the door and relocked it before leading the way along the hall to the kitchen.

"I just brewed tea," he said carelessly. "Care for a cup?"

"I would, thank you." For some reason Eliot found himself adopting a somewhat formal tone with this man.

Malone pointed to one of the kitchen chairs. "So sit."

Eliot sat. Malone put two cups on the table, got a strainer, and filled them with steaming, dark tea. In the daylight, Eliot saw for the first time the deep lines gouged into Malone's tough face. But he saw, too, the breadth of his chest and the way muscle bulged the sleeves of his wool shirt.

"Care for a nip of something stronger in the tea?" Malone asked.

"No, thanks."

"Well, I would." Malone got a whiskey bottle from the cupboard, opened it, and poured a shot into his own tea. "You one of those who think liquor's the Devil's brew?"

"I used to like a drink once in a while," Eliot told him. "But it's against the law right now, and I'm a Prohibition agent."

"I won't tell."

"Better if I keep the habit of not drinking. That way I won't forget and take one with witnesses around." Eliot's smile was rueful. "Never know when there's some news photographer close by."

Malone almost smiled. Almost. "Yeah, that one really caught you with your pants down in that raid." He took a big swallow of his spiked tea, not flinching at its heat. "Now, what do you want?"

Eliot took a small sip of his own tea. But it was still too hot even for sipping. He put his cup down. "I told you. I need help."

Malone leaned back in his chair and took out his key chain with the medallion. He fiddled with it between the fingers of his left hand. "I'm just a poor beat cop. How can I help you?"

"Work with me. I've spoken to the U.S. district attorney. The Justice Department can arrange a temporary transfer from police duty for you, deputize you to assist me."

"Why should I, though?"

"Because you're what I need—a good cop."

"How do you know that?"

"You told me. That night by the bridge. By what you said and how you acted. And what I sensed in you."

Malone regarded him sardonically. "You a good judge of character?"

"Fair."

"I'm such a good cop, how come I'm walkin' a beat? At my age?"

"You want to tell me?"

"Well," Malone said archly, "maybe I'm that Whore with a Heart of Gold we hear about but seldom come across. Maybe I'm the Good Cop in a Bad Town. That what you want to hear?"

Eliot tried another sip of tea. It burned a bit less than the previous try. "All right," he said, "I'll tell you why you're still walking a beat. Because there've been a couple of interruptions to your police career. First the war, and recovering from the wounds you got in it along with some very important medals."

Malone frowned at him. "You've been researching me," he said accusingly but not quite angrily.

"Then when you went back on the force you got into trouble. Caught a couple of Capone gorillas killing a hood from a rival mob. You shot one of them dead, but the other got away—after shooting you."

Malone touched a blunt fingertip to his chest, his expression somewhat nostalgic. "The doctors decided it was safer not to take the lead out. It wanders around in there, hurts sometimes."

"You recognized the one who shot you and identified him before you passed out. But the Capone organization put in some high-up pressure. A superior officer came to see you in the hospital. Suggested you change your mind about that identification. You refused. So he went back and told a judge you weren't in any physical or mental shape to make your identification of that Capone gunman stick. The judge quickly and obligingly dismissed the charges before you were well enough to appear and say your piece in person."

Malone regarded him and remained silent, and took another swig of his spiked tea.

Eliot tried his again. It was just right now. "When you did get out of the hospital, you filed departmental charges against that superior officer."

"Didn't hurt *his* career any. He got promoted."

"And you've stayed a beat cop ever since. With a number of people who don't like or trust you. Including some on the police force, as well as in the rackets. They marked you 'not cooperative.' I guess that's another way of saying you're too honest."

"Or too stupid-stubborn. I'll grant one thing—you did a thorough research job. But what's it leading up to?"

Eliot finished his tea and said, "I'll tell you."

Malone regarded him with mild curiosity, nothing more, and waited.

"Another thing I learned about you," Eliot told him. "You've been around a long time. And your father was a cop before you. Starting with what he gave you, and what you've added since, you've got one of the best informer networks in Chicago."

"Not professional informers," Malone corrected flatly. "People I've gotten to know. Friends. Or anyway people who know they can trust me. In a lot of places. The kind that can find out what's going on for me. If I push hard enough. Make 'em realize I want to know real bad."

"That's the kind of network I need," Eliot said softly.

"I'm not giving you any of mine, get that straight."

"Why not?"

"You *had* an informer. You got him killed."

Eliot fought down a surge of anger at this man. But Malone saw it flare briefly in Eliot's eyes. He went on with it relentlessly, as though trying to find out if he could provoke an outburst. "You didn't keep your informant a secret, and somebody heard about it and had him murdered."

But Eliot was calm again. "Then come in with me and keep your informants secret. I'll never ask who or what any of them are. Just use them. To help me do the job."

"No."

Eliot repeated the question. "Why not?"

"Because I don't feel like playing in your game. Tennis—that was your game in college, right? Tough player, won a lot."

"You've been checking up on me, too, it seems."

"I got curious. The point is, Mr. Ness, this isn't a *game* you can play with Big Al. Oh, you can win—in a way, maybe. Like if you bother him enough maybe he'll give you a chunk of dough to stop doing it. That's one way of winning a game, I guess. I just never learned. Too stupid."

Eliot stabbed a finger at him, letting the anger show plainly now. "I studied business in college, *Mister* Malone. If money was my most important goal I'd have gone into business. Instead I became an investigator. A kind of cop. You could ask why. I'd say because I like this kind of combat. I like a fight, and I like to win. I like to *beat* my opponent. If you take his money to lose the game, he beats you."

"But he wouldn't kill you, if the game's tennis. Refuse a Capone offer and he *will* kill you. Because for his kind, offering a bribe's trying to handle you the nice way. Say no and there's only two things he knows to do about it next. Break you or kill you."

"Is that what he did?" Eliot said softly. "Broke you?"

Malone's big hands closed into fists. Then he took a deep breath and opened them again. "This is a game you're trying to play on a field that already belongs to Capone. Or close enough. You can't win it."

"I need your help. I'm asking you for help."

"And I'm turning you down. Maybe if I'd met you ten

years and twenty pounds ago...But now...I guess it's just gotten more important to me to stay alive. It's called *fear*, Mr. Ness."

"A man who becomes a cop," Eliot said, "knows going in he may have to risk his life for the job."

"Sure. But that's with the idea your fellow cops and the courts are with you. That they'll revenge your death by punishing whoever murdered you. That gives you a feeling of being part of something—and of purpose, even in dying. But that's not what happens when a cop gets shot in Chicago. Not anymore. Letting yourself get in the way of being murdered, when you know it won't even serve any purpose—that's not what I joined the department for."

Eliot studied Malone's face. At last he nodded.

Malone's eyes narrowed to slits. "What's that mean?"

"It means I do understand what you're saying." Eliot stood up. "Thanks for the tea and your time."

After he was gone, James Malone walked into his living room and stood looking at the three framed photographs on the mantel.

His young bride, in her wedding gown. His mother, in her Sunday best. His father, in his uniform.

His family. All gone. Leaving him alone. And he was sometimes not pleasant company for himself.

He went on looking at them—but hearing again that question Eliot Ness had asked him:

Is that what Capone did? Broke you?

TWELVE

Cora was already half asleep on the sofa when "Amos 'n' Andy" finished that evening and Catherine turned off the radio. Eliot lifted his daughter and set her on her feet. "Okay, honey, time to go up with Mommy and get ready for bed. I'll be up to kiss you goodnight soon as you're tucked in."

As Catherine took Cora's hand the little girl looked speculatively at her mother's swollen belly. "Mommy, when is my little brother going to come?"

Catherine laughed and patted herself. "Soon, Cora. Only it *could* turn out to be a little sister."

"I don't want one of those. I want a *brother*."

Eliot grinned and pointed at the stairs. "You'll take what you get—like Mommy and me. Now scoot!"

When Catherine and Cora vanished at the top of the stairway, Eliot's grin dissolved and the tiredness settled in. The tiredness of frustration, more than anything else. He went to the living-room window and stared out at the shadowed street.

Had he given up on Malone too soon, too easily? Was there something more he could have done or said to change Malone's mind?

Eliot pictured the set of Malone's lined, hard face and shook his head. No. There was one thing Malone had proved beyond any doubt in his life: he was not a man you could push or cajole into doing anything he'd decided not to.

Stupid-stubborn, that's how Malone had described himself. Stupid he definitely was not. But the stubborn part: solid rock.

Eliot knew there was no point in coming up with further arguments. He'd tried with him and couldn't have him. He would just have to find someone else—some other way.

When he entered his office at headquarters next morning, Eliot found a dumpy, fortyish man with bifocals sitting in the corner chair to the left of his desk.

The man jumped to his feet, smiling at Eliot uncertainly. "Mr. Ness? I'm Oscar Wallace—from Washington? The department sent me out here to lend you a hand with Capone."

Eliot shook the extended hand, looking Oscar Wallace over dubiously. This didn't look like a man you could feel all that secure having at your side when it came to trading blows with a bootleg mob.

But you couldn't always judge by a man's looks, which could be deceiving. And the department surely wouldn't have sent him here to tackle Capone's Chicago unless he had something not immediately apparent to offer.

"Well, Mr. Wallace," Eliot told him, "I can certainly use some help with it, and that's a fact. So I can sincerely say I'm pleased to have you. Frankly, I seem to be doing a little stumbling around in the dark at the moment. Any fresh ideas would be most welcome, if you've brought any with you."

"Yes, sir, I did," Wallace assured him, with a confidence undermined by a somewhat squeaky voice. "And the one I want to try first is this—Capone has not made a return since 1926."

Eliot didn't understand. "A return?"

"An income tax return. He hasn't filed one in five years."

Eliot stared at the man. "Income tax," he repeated flatly.

"Yessir." Oscar Wallace was obviously puzzled by Eliot's expression.

"Mr. Wallace, excuse me but . . . what is it you do at the department?"

"I'm an accountant."

Eliot half sighed, half laughed. "An accountant."

"Yes, sir. The department has sent me out here to—"

"Would you excuse me, please, Mr. Wallace?" Eliot interrupted, poker-faced. "I forgot I have a short appointment upstairs this morning. Just make yourself comfortable, I'll be back soon."

"Sure, no trouble." Wallace was settling back down in the chair as Eliot walked out of the office.

Halfway down the hall, Eliot stopped, lit a cigarette, and leaned his shoulders against the wall, rubbing his forehead. Was this some kind of joke? What did the department think they were dealing with out here?

An *accountant*. Eliot had half an urge to go back in there and ask Oscar Wallace if he was good with guns— just to watch him come apart. He rubbed his eyes, telling himself to simmer down.

When he took his hand away from his eyes he saw James Malone standing at the other end of the hall, looking his way.

He wasn't in uniform. A rakish cloth cap. Aging

tweed jacket over a knitted tan cardigan. Dark brown wool trousers.

Eliot walked down the hall to him. When he was very close Malone said softly, "Come on."

"Where are we going?"

"These walls have ears," Malone told him. Taking a grip on Eliot's arm, he marched him out of the headquarters building.

The church was two blocks away. The only other person inside it at that time of the morning was an old woman down front who was lighting a candle and saying a prayer.

Malone settled Eliot and himself down in the rear. "You told me yesterday you wanted to know how to get Capone. Do you *really* want to get him?"

"I told you I do, and I meant it."

"Did you, now?" Malone grimaced slightly. "You don't see what I'm sayin', do you? What are you prepared to do in order to get him?"

"Everything within the law," Eliot told him.

"And *then* what are you prepared to do, after that?" Malone's shrewd-mean eyes probed Eliot's. "Y'see, if you open the ball on these people, Mr. Ness, you've got to be prepared to go all the way. And that could turn out to be as long a way as there is, in this world or the next. Because once it starts, *they* will not stop the fight till one of you is dead."

Eliot's heart seemed to be beating faster, as though it was being revved up by some force coming out of Malone. He had to concentrate to keep his voice down. "I want to get Capone. I don't know *how* to get him."

"Well, I'll tell you. You want to get Capone, here's how you go about it. He pulls a knife, you pull a gun. He sends one of your people to the hospital, you send one of his to the morgue. That's the Chicago way." The intensity of Malone's voice seemed greater for its quietness.

"You got to break some rules and regulations. Maybe a lot of 'em. Now—do you want to do that? Are you ready to do that?"

Malone leaned closer and his voice became a whisper. "You understand what I'm doin'? I'm offering you a deal. You want this deal?"

"I have sworn," Eliot said in as level a voice as he could manage before all that intensity of Malone's, "I've sworn to put that man away, with any and all legal means at my disposal. And I will do so."

"All *legal* means..." Malone repeated caustically, and then heaved a sigh. "Well, the Lord hates a coward."

Ceremoniously, James Malone extended his hand. With equal gravity, Eliot Ness seized and shook it.

"You know what a blood oath is?" Malone asked in a suddenly more relaxed tone.

"Yes."

"Well, you just took one. Let's go take a walk. I need to work off some steam."

As they strolled along the street together, Malone asked Eliot, "How do you figure Capone knew about your raid on his warehouse the other night?"

Eliot didn't like saying it, but he did. "I think someone on the cops told him."

Malone actually grinned at him, though it was not the most pleasant of grins. "And welcome to Chicago, mister. Now you're beginning to get it. 'Cause this town stinks like a levee whorehouse at low tide." Malone looked up at the sky and filled his lungs with air, as though he was beginning to enjoy himself. "Now, the first thing is—who can you trust?"

"I—"

Malone interrupted him. "You can trust *nobody*. The cops—*nobody*. Nobody wants you here in this town. Get that through your noggin."

"Then why are *you* helping me?"

"Because I swore to uphold the law. And if you believe that one I'll tell you another. Now then, who can you trust?"

Eliot said it grimly: "I can trust nobody."

Malone nodded, satisfied. "And that, my friend, is the sorry truth."

"But if we can trust nobody," Eliot pointed out, "where do we get help?"

"When you're afraid of getting a rotten apple, don't take it out of the barrel—get it off the tree." Malone stuck two fingers between his teeth and let out a whistle that brought a taxicab from half a block away.

"Let's you and me go take a look at that tree."

THIRTEEN

Eliot described Oscar Wallace, the man who had just arrived from Washington to help fight Capone, as Malone led the way through the ground floor of the Police Academy.

Malone shook his head unbelievingly. "They sent you an *accountant*?"

"My sentiments, exactly."

"There's a real good journalist wrote an account last year of Capone's takeover of this town—so far." Malone opened a door and they started down a stairway to the basement area under the academy. "He had the perfect title ready for anybody who does a history of however it finally ends up."

"What?"

"The Moving Trigger-Finger Writes."

"Trigger-finger . . . Well, that's why we're here."

Malone opened a heavy, soundproofed door. They stepped through into the Police Academy's shooting range and were immediately engulfed by the noise and fumes of multiple gunfire.

A dozen new, very young recruits in Police Academy sweatshirts were lined up firing revolvers at their targets. Two other groups of twelve stood to one side awaiting their turns. The noise abruptly ceased as the dozen on the firing line used up the last of their ammunition. The rangemaster, a scowling police instructor in his forties, barked commands at them: "Finger outta the trigger guard. *Eject* those cartridges. Lay the revolver on the ledge, pick up your target, and stand back."

The recruits obeyed and stepped back from the firing line. At the rangemaster's next command the targets they'd been shooting at came forward on their pulley wires and each young marksman picked up his own. Eye-stinging gunsmoke drifted thickly in the windlowless room.

"Left face and file off," the rangemaster snapped at the recruits as Eliot and Malone approached him. "Next group of twelve—stand ready!"

He was about to give the next command when Eliot stepped in front of him and introduced himself. "I'm Eliot Ness, Treasury Department. We require a recruit for extended special duty. Because there's likely to be extreme danger involved in the assignment, I don't want any married candidates. The recruit we choose will be seconded to the department, under my command."

Eliot produced a folded document from inside his jacket. "As you'll see here, we have the full cooperation of the United States district attorney here in Chicago."

But the rangemaster wasn't paying any attention to him. He was punching James Malone playfully on the shoulder, his scowl giving way to a grin. "Hey, Jimmy, long time no see. What're you doing around here outta uniform?"

"Tryin' to get a feel of the civilian outlook on life, Joey. How's your sister?"

"She still keeps askin' when you're gonna come around for dinner again. I try to make her understand, you ain't never gonna marry again. Not her or anybody else."

"Not likely," Malone agreed. "Tell me, Joey, who's the best shot you got among all these new kids?"

"We got two real prodigies in this year's bunch—Williamson and Stone."

"Will ya send 'em over to us, Joey? One at a time."

"Sure. Williamson's in the group that just fired. I'll have him show you his target, so you can see. But Stone's just as good. Toss-up."

As the rangemaster crossed to the young recruits, Malone looked curiously at Eliot. "Don't want any that're married, eh."

"The way things are shaping up, I don't want to be worrying about making anybody's wife a widow."

"*You're* married."

"I know."

"Any kids?"

"One. Another due in about a month."

"Aren't you worried about leaving *them* without a husband and father?"

"Yes," Eliot said, "I am."

Malone was still regarding him curiously when one of the recruits walked over to them. He was tall and lean, with pale yellow hair and neatly chiseled features.

"Williamson?" Eliot asked.

"Yes, sir." Williamson came to attention before him, holding his clipboard in one hand and target in the other.

"Can I see your target?"

Williamson showed it. The shots he'd fired had made a single large jagged hole in the ten ring.

"Impressive," Eliot said.

"Thank you, sir."

"Stand easy, pal," Malone told the recruit. "I want to ask you something. Why do you want to join the force?"

Williamson looked disconcerted. "Why...?" He paused and thought about it, with frowning concentration.

"Don't search for the yearbook answer, just tell me. I want *your* reason."

"Well, because I...ummm..." Williamson fell silent again, trying to figure out the right thing to say.

"Okay," Malone told him, not unkindly, "that's all, kid."

Williamson, still frowning, retreated back to his group of recruits.

"Bullets ain't enough," Malone muttered. "Gotta have some brains, too."

The rangemaster was barking at the recruits again. "Next group of twelve. Advance to the firing line. Lay your revolver and three rounds on the ledge. Do *not* load until the command. Advance." When this group was lined up and ready, he gave the command: "*Load.*"

Malone and Eliot walked over to him. "Let's see your other prodigy, Joey," Malone said.

The rangemaster snapped, "Stone."

One of the recruits at the firing line put the revolver he'd just loaded down beside his clipboard and turned. He was about twenty, with a dark, intense face dominated by a jutting nose and almost-black eyes. And he was so short Eliot was sure the boy had barely managed to squeeze past the police department's height regulations.

Eliot and Malone walked along the recruit line to him. "Why do you want to become a cop?" Malone asked him without preamble.

The answer came back fast and smooth: "To protect the property and citizenry of the city of Chi—"

Malone cut him off. "Don't waste my time with that kind of *bullshit*."

The short, dark recruit smiled a little. "Gotten by with it pretty well so far, around here in the academy."

This one, Eliot thought, did have brains.

But Malone was scowling at the recruit, his eyes at their meanest. "Stone . . . that's your name?"

"Yes, sir."

Malone glanced down at Stone's clipboard. "George Stone," he read aloud. His eyes snapped back to Stone's face. "What's your real name?"

"That's my real name, sir."

"What was it before you changed it?"

"I didn't change it." There was an edge of defensive defiance in Stone's voice. "My father did, when he came over from the old country. Immigration officer said he ought to, so he wouldn't sound like a foreigner. He was afraid he wouldn't get in if he didn't so he went along with it. I'm named after him. Giuseppe Petri."

"That's what I thought," Malone said caustically. He looked at Eliot. "That's all we need, a sneaky wop bastard along."

The black eyes narrowed. "*What?*"

"Ever heard of an Irishman changing his name?" Malone rasped. "No, because we're not ashamed of what we are. But all you dago scum have to hide what—"

Stone said softly, "I don't like to beat up on a broken-down old man, not even when he's an Irish pig. But you use that stinkin' Mick mouth on me again and I'm gonna—"

Malone's hand went to his back pocket and whipped out a blackjack. "You scum, I'm gonna break your head!"

Just as fast, Stone snatched his revolver off the firing ledge and stood ready for Malone's attack. "Come on, Paddy."

Malone returned the blackjack to his back pocket and told Eliot, "I like him."

"I do, too."

Stone was slowly putting his gun back down on the ledge, looking stunned.

The rangemaster grinned at him. "Relax, Stone. My old friend Jimmy was testing you a little—and I think you passed."

Stone looked from him back to Malone, still a bit shaken.

"Son," Malone told him, "you just joined the Treasury Department."

FOURTEEN

Malone's expression was a thin, cynical smile. Beside him, Stone's was polite, noncommittal attention. They sat on a bench near the gun rack on the side wall of Eliot's office, listening silently while Lieutenant Alderson explained the folders he was placing on the desk.

"This one," he was telling Eliot, "contains the reports from our flying squad surveillances in Chicago Heights. They've located six different speakeasies in that area so far. And this last report is from the stakeout on that garage on the West Side. Still no proof the trucks in there are used to transport liquor. But whenever they move out they'll be tailed. If they do pick up liquor or beer, that'll give us the places they get it from."

Eliot nodded at the folders. "Well, everybody's certainly been out there keeping busy."

"The men are all trying their best, Mr. Ness. Any new orders?"

"No, not at the moment. Thank you, Lieutenant."

Alderson looked curiously at Malone and Stone, obviously waiting for a formal introduction. When none was forthcoming, he nodded stiffly and left the office.

After he'd gone Eliot tapped the reports on his desk and looked at Malone. "Well, what do you think of these?"

"I think there's nothing like vaudeville," Malone told him in a bored voice. "Six speakeasies they found—hell, all you got to do to locate speaks is take a walk down almost any street. There must be over two thousand of 'em in Chicago, not to mention Cicero and other outlying communities. You could knock over a couple of them every day and it wouldn't bother Capone. Not enough liquor in any of them at any time to cost him the kind of dough he'd notice."

"Every time speaks get closed in my neighborhood," Stone said, placing his palms flat together to illustrate, "they just open again next door or next block." He spread his hands apart, then swung a hand back in between. "Or reopen in the same place—after a court order by one of Capone's tame judges."

"Kid," Malone told him, "if you want to pass as a George Stone instead of a Giuseppe Petri you got to learn how to talk without using your hands."

"And if you want to pass as a half-intelligent old man," Stone countered evenly, "you got to learn to stop using that phony Mick brogue."

Malone's laugh was the first genuine one Eliot had heard from the big, bitter cop. "You got another problem, kid," Malone told Stone. "No respect for your elders."

Eliot was still looking at the reports Lieutenant Alderson had left on his desk, only half listening to their exchange of insults. "You're right, of course. Hitting speakeasies won't accomplish what we want. We have to find people who can hunt out the more important places for us. The liquor warehouses, big stills, and breweries. Places we can strip Capone of enough stuff to lose him the kind of money that *will* bother him."

"Plenty of people know where the booze is," Malone said. "That's not the problem. The problem is finding the people who know *and* can get up the nerve to cross Capone. I've got my feelers out to some of those. Some friends that think they'll be locating a still Capone has somewhere along the Levee pretty soon. And a big brewery in Cicero."

Malone stood up and flexed his big shoulders. "But why wait? If you're ready to go to work, I know a place we could raid right now. Don't even need cars. We can walk it. Less than two blocks from headquarters here."

Eliot's blood quickened. "What is it?"

"Liquor storeplace. Not big, but all the stuff in it's first class. Worth a *lot*. No rotgut or bathtub gin. Imported goodies—and not the kind's been cut three ways and rebottled, either. The stuff in this place is strictly for Capone's carriage trade."

Eliot stood up, grinning. "Let's go do some good."

"We could use one more man along," Malone said. "If we just had somebody else we could trust to—"

At that point Oscar Wallace waddled into the office, carrying a heavy opened ledger in both arms. "Mr. Ness, the financial disbursement pattern I've been trying to put together—"

Malone interrupted. "You—*Accountant*—have you ever done any shootin'?"

Wallace blinked through his bifocals, puzzled. "Shooting?"

"Shooting."

"When I was younger. My father used to take me hunting with him. Never liked it, though—killing innocent animals for sport, it made me feel sick. Since he's been gone, I only go out in the country sometimes, to do a little plinking."

It was Malone's turn to stare. "Plinking?"

Wallace nodded. "You know, shooting tin cans and bottles. Just target practice, with my old .22 rifle."

Malone took a riot gun and a box of ammunition for it from the rack on the side wall, loaded the weapon, and handed it to Oscar Wallace. "Stick it under your coat and come along."

Wallace was blinking again. "Along where . . . what?"

"A liquor raid."

"But, I . . . uh . . ."

"You carry a badge?"

"Well, yes."

"Carry a gun." Malone strode out of the office with Eliot, followed by Stone. Wallace, after another second's hesitation, shrugged to himself, hid the riot gun under his coat, held it there between his arm and side, and brought up the rear.

They went down the stairway to the ground floor and were walking through the hallway toward the headquarters entrance when Deputy Chief Mike Casey came out of the front elevator and saw them. He stopped, staring at Malone.

"*Jimmy*—what're you doing around here out of uniform? You dressed for Halloween or something?"

"My new working clothes, Mike."

Eliot told Casey, "Malone's been transferred to me for a while, by order of the Justice Department. I see you two know each other."

Casey smiled. "Since a long way back. We used to walk a beat together."

Malone said, deadpan, "Only you've done a lot better for yourself since."

"You deserved to do better, too, Jimmy. Just ran into lousy luck."

"That what you'd call it, Mike? Lousy luck?"

"Looks like that's changing, though. You *could* do very well for yourself, now you're an assistant fed."

"Nice chatting with you," Malone told Casey, "but we gotta go."

"Where you going?"

"You'll be hearing about it," Malone said, and led the way out to the street.

As he'd said, it wasn't far to walk. Across the first intersection and another half block. Then he turned into a post office.

Eliot, coming in after him with Stone and Wallace, asked, "What are we doing here?"

"Like I said. Liquor raid."

Eliot, puzzled, glanced around the post office. "In *here*?"

"You got it." Malone nodded toward a door in the side wall. "See that door? If you walk through there with me now, you are walking into a world of trouble—and there'll be no turning back. You understand me?"

"Yes. I do."

"Then let's get to it. Do some good, like you're fond of saying."

The four of them crossed the post office to the closed side door. Malone poised his left hand an inch from the knob. "If it's unlocked," Malone told them softly, "I go *straight* through. If it's locked I kick it open and then go through—*straight*." To Eliot he said, "You swing in soon's you can squeeze by me and cover anybody who's to my right." To Stone he said, "Swing and cover to the left."

He told Wallace, "You cover my back—until we're sure nobody's coming in after us. Then fast turn and do whatever looks necessary. Got that?"

The dumpy accountant nodded, one time, as though that movement was difficult because his neck muscles were paralyzed. He didn't say anything because his teeth were locked shut.

Malone reached inside his jacket and around to his

back. He tugged a snub-nosed .38 from the belt holster there, but kept it out of sight under his jacket. Then he seized the doorknob, turned it fast, and pushed.

It wasn't locked. Malone took two long strides through it—into a wide corridor that ran the length of the building in either direction, bringing his .38 up pointing straight ahead. Eliot swung through a split second later, turning his back to Malone's right side and aiming his .45 automatic down the corridor in that direction. Stone swung in at the same time, bringing a service revolver out of a concealed hip holster and pointing it along the left extension of the corridor. Wallace backed in after them, dragging the riot gun from under his coat and shutting the door behind them.

There was nobody at all anywhere in the corridor to shoot at or worry about.

"Saints be praised," Malone whispered. "We got lucky. Somebody's been careless—no outside guard."

There was another closed door almost directly across the corridor. He nodded at it. "Same attack positions for each of us going through this one."

He didn't bother checking if this door was locked, quite sure it would be. Sticking the snub-nosed .38 in the front of his belt, Malone took a fire ax down off its wall brackets. With one mighty swing he chopped into the door close to its handle, ripping a hole through it. Dropping the ax, Malone accomplished several things at the same time, very fast. He got the .38 back in his right fist. His left hand went through the hole and opened the inside lock. His heavy-soled, hard-toed right shoe kicked the door wide open.

Then he was barging straight inside, shouting, "Federal officers! This is a raid!"

Eliot swung in to his right, Stone to the left, and Wallace brought up the rear.

They were inside a very large storeroom, almost filled with stacks of big crates piled to the very high ceiling. In the back three men were at work removing bottles of British whiskey and French champagne from big crates and putting them in smaller ones for delivery to Capone's "carriage trade."

In front, to either side of the kicked-open door, two burly guards had been lounging in chairs with tommy guns on their laps. They leaped up when the first three invaders burst in—but neither got a chance to use his weapon.

Eliot slugged the one on the right unconscious with his .45 and strode past his falling figure to cover the workmen in the rear.

The other guard let his tommy gun fall to the floor when he found himself looking cross-eyed into the muzzle of Stone's revolver, aimed at the bridge of his nose at a distance of less than three inches. Stone began backing him toward the rear.

All this had happened so fast Oscar Wallace had still not finished coming through the kicked-open door.

A barrel-shaped bruiser stepped out of a bathroom door behind Malone. He had an entirely bald head and bushy eyebrows. He also had a pistol, which he started to bring to bear on Malone's back.

He didn't complete the move because Oscar Wallace jumped forward and jammed the very large mouth of his riot gun against his ear.

"Drop it!" Wallace squeaked. "*Please*! Or I'll blow your head off!"

The bruiser with the bald head and bushy eyebrows opened his hand and the pistol dropped, bouncing away across the floorboards. By then Malone had turned around. He regarded the man with what seemed to be an expression of pure pleasure.

"This is a private business establishment," the bruiser said uncertainly. "What are you people doing breaking in here?"

Malone stepped close to him. "It's simple. Everything in this place is impounded and you're all under arrest."

"You can't come in like this unless you got a warrant," the barrel-shaped bruiser protested. "You *got* a warrant?"

"Here's my warrant," Malone said, and drove his left fist viciously into the man's stomach.

The man went to his knees, gagging, clutching at his middle and lowering his head to the floor.

Malone looked down at him and murmured, "How d'you think he feels now, better or worse?"

Eliot and Stone came from the rear, shepherding the rest of the men they'd caught in the place. "Search them while Stone keeps them covered," Eliot told Wallace. "When we're sure they're disarmed you'll have to go round us up a lot of handcuffs and a couple of trucks big enough to carry away all this stuff."

"Well, Mr. Ness," Malone said, "we're in for it now. I guess you know that."

Eliot nodded cheerfully. "Must be nearly two hundred thousand dollars worth of Capone merchandise we'll be taking out of here. He won't shrug *that* off. Scared?"

"Might be," Malone said, "when I get time to think about it. Right now, I got to admit, I'm feeling pretty good."

There were two dinners held that night, in two far-separated parts of the city—both occasioned by the successful raid on Capone's carriage trade liquor supply.

One was hosted by Eliot Ness. The other by Al Capone.

The mood and purpose of the two were strikingly different.

FIFTEEN

One was held in an Italian restaurant called the Little Capri. It was a celebration dinner for the four of them: Eliot Ness, James Malone, George Stone, and Oscar Wallace. They ate heartily, savoring their victory, each having reason to feel pleased with himself.

As their meal reached its end Eliot opened a box of cigars he'd bought for the occasion and passed it around their table. Each man took one, though none was normally a cigar smoker. A cigar was the traditional way to cap a special festive evening.

Malone took out his key chain and used the point of the key to pierce his cigar end.

Eliot looked at the medallion at the other end of the short chain. "I keep wondering—what *is* that?"

"What is it?" Malone repeated, in some outrage. "What *is* it, the man asks me. Have I fallen among the Heathen? It's my callbox key—and Saint Jude."

Stone frowned at the medallion. "Saint Jude?"

"Saint Jude," Malone told them, "is the patron of lost causes and policemen."

Eliot could not be sure if Malone was revealing a sentimental streak or being ironical.

Oscar Wallace, blowing a cloud of cigar smoke at the ceiling, repeated reflectively, "The patron of policemen."

Malone raised and lowered his big shoulders in a slow shrug. "Everybody needs a friend."

Everyone nodded in solemn agreement with that.

"And you," Malone said, fixing his gaze on Stone, "when you go back to the *Academy*—of Lost Causes and Policemen—which one do *you* want to be?"

"I want to be a cop."

"You *do*?"

"Yes."

"And why?"

Stone promptly recited his foolproof Police Academy answer: "To protect the property and citizenry of—"

Malone cut in with a groan. "Dear Lord, the boy has no shame at all." He leaned toward Stone, planting his elbows on the table. "Well, I'm gonna tell you a very important thing you're gonna find out for yourself one day. Lost causes and policemen: sometimes they're the same, and sometimes they're not. And sometimes you're goin' to find yourself in a situation where you have to choose which of those you're goin' to be."

He seemed to be saying this last more to himself. And having said it, he leaned back and lit his cigar, apparently not requiring or wanting a response.

At that moment the waiter, who spoke very little English, came in bearing a tray with a bottle and four glasses on it. He addressed himself in rapid Italian to Stone, who translated for the other three men at the table:

"He says it's on the house—a nice glass of grappa to wash our food down."

Eliot sighed a bit. "Tell him thank you, but I don't think so. Not for me."

Stone translated that to the waiter, who looked perplexed at Eliot and then asked Stone an equally perplexed question.

"He says," Stone told Eliot, "that if you don't like grappa, what *do* you want to end the meal?"

"Tell him I'd like some tea," Eliot said with a slight smile.

Stone looked a bit puzzled too as he translated that into Italian and then gave Eliot the waiter's astonished response. "He can't understand why anybody'd want to wind up a good meal with *tea*."

"Tell him because it's the Cup that Cheers—like they say in the radio commercials."

Malone laughed softly. "I got to say one thing for you, Mr. Ness. You got the nerve to stick to a decision, no matter how silly it makes you seem. Stupid-stubborn, like me."

Oscar Wallace piped up, "I'll have a cup of tea, too."

"And so will I," Malone conceded, and looked at Stone. "And I guess you'd better, too. You see, Mr. Ness takes being a Treasury officer seriously, and it would embarrass him to get caught doing some illegal drinking in public. And since you and me are part of his team right now..."

It was Stone's turn to be embarrassed as he told the waiter to take the grappa back, they all would prefer tea. The waiter looked at them as if they were crazy, gave a helpless shrug, and carried the tray back into the kitchen.

"I'll tell you one thing, Mr. Ness," Stone said, "don't expect me to eat my meals without wine at *home*. My parents would never understand. They'd figure I suddenly turned into some kind of degenerate."

Malone looked to Oscar Wallace. "You drink, in the privacy of your home?"

"No," Wallace told him, "I never do."

"*Never*?"

"No."

"Worried about your morals—or your health?"

"My sanity, perhaps," Wallace said quietly. After a moment he added simply, with no outward show of emotion, "My mother was an alcoholic. I used to watch my father trying to control her when she had the DTs and thought ants were crawling all over her face and hands. Until I was ten. That's when she died of it."

It was the first time Eliot had known James Malone to have nothing to say.

Eliot got home that night in time to stand in the doorway of his daughter's bedroom and hear the end of her prayers. When she reached "Amen," Catherine, seated on the edge of Cora's bed, repeated it and then kissed her.

"Goodnight, Mommy."

"Goodnight," Catherine whispered, and rose from the child's bed.

Cora looked toward her doorway. "Goodnight, Daddy."

Eliot came in and bent to kiss her. "Goodnight, little girl. Sleep tight."

She giggled sleepily. "And don't let the bedbugs bite?"

"That's right. Now close your eyes and have sweet dreams." Eliot turned off the lamp and followed Catherine out of the room, closing the door softly behind them.

Out in the hallway Catherine asked him, keeping her voice down, "Was the celebration dinner nice?"

Eliot nodded. "They're good men. Suprisingly good. Each in his own way."

They walked down the hallway. When they reached the stairs Eliot turned to go down to his study. Catherine stopped him. "Where are you going?"

"I've got some things to prepare for tomorrow."

"You've had a pretty full day already, it seems to me."

"Yes, I certainly did."

"And you've still got some energy left?"

"Lots of work to do."

Catherine smiled and took his hand. "Why don't you come in and brush my hair?" She glanced down at her distended belly and added, "Or am I getting too unattractive for—"

He silenced her with a kiss. It turned into a lingering one. When her lips parted from his, she led him into their bedroom, shaking her head.

"*You* . . ." Her voice was somewhere between a growl and a purr. ". . . *detective*."

The dinner Al Capone staged that night took place much later, in the banquet room of the Lexington Hotel. It wasn't a celebration dinner. None of the other men seated around the long table with Capone were quite sure *what* it was supposed to be.

No outsiders were present in the room. The doors had been closed and locked after the last serving. Capone sat at the head of the table, apparently enjoying himself, digging lustily into his third heaping plateful of food and washing it down with copious amounts of wine. His bookkeeper, Walter Payne, was at the other end of the table from him. Seated along both long sides of the table were more of his closest aides, plus some of his most proven enforcers and bodyguards. Men like Vince Matranga, Frank Nitti, Machine-Gun McGurn, Frankie Rio.

And Jock Miller, the barrel-shaped bruiser with the bald head and bushy eyebrows that Malone had gut-punched in the raided liquor storeroom.

He was drinking a lot, but he hadn't eaten anything. His throat was too tight to get food down. Because he kept wondering why he was here.

He had been bailed out of jail quickly after the raid, along with the others who'd been arrested. But none of the others had been invited to this dinner. And that worried Jock Miller—it *scared* him.

The case against him and the others out on bail, Jock Miller knew, would get dropped by one of the judges on Capone's payroll. It would never go to court, where the questions and answers might prove embarrassing to Capone.

But there was no way of getting back all that expensive liquor the raiders had taken away. By sometime tomorrow every bottle would be smashed, their contents poured down the sewers. Capone couldn't take that big a loss lightly. Yet there he sat at the head of the table, appearing entirely relaxed as he finished his big meal. And he seemed to accept Jock Miller's explanation of the failure to keep out the federal raiders.

When Capone's plate was empty he pushed it aside, thumped his belly contentedly, took a last swallow of wine—and looked along the table at Jock Miller. The look was friendly enough. Capone's voice sounded friendly, too, but a bit puzzled.

"I been thinking about it, Jock, and I still can't understand it. There was only four feds on the raid. Three with handguns, one with a riot gun. Okay. I had three guards on that place. Two inside with tommy guns, one out in the corridor standing watch. All the guy outside had to do was give one rap on the door when he saw the feds come through the post office, to warn the two inside so they'd have time to get set. If they'd been ready, those two could've chopped the four feds to ribbons with the tommy guns before they got halfway through the door."

Drops of perspiration ran down Jock Miller's face. His clothes felt drenched. "I *told* you, Al, I—"

"Yeah," Capone cut in, "you did tell me. It was your turn on watch out there in the corridor. Only you had to go inside to take a leak." Capone laughed. "Well, that's normal. Guy's gotta go, he's gotta go. Me, you, anybody. Understandable. What I don't understand, Jock, is why you didn't send one a the other guys outside to stand watch while you took that leak."

"It was only for a *minute*," Jock Miller blurted, the fear making his voice shrill. "I didn't think we had to go to all that bother for just a minute. Christ, Al, there's *never* been any trouble at all at that place. The kind of protection you've got on it, who'd expect *anybody* to ever hit it?"

"That's true," Capone acknowledged slowly. He leaned back in his chair, considering, and then repeated. "True. Who'd expect it? Nobody." He sighed and shook his head. "It's a loss—a disappointment—but it's done and over with. Life goes on." Capone shrugged. "Okay, I ain't gonna spend the rest of my life feeling bad about it. I like to *enjoy* life, everybody here knows *that*, eh?"

Capone's gaze was no longer fixed on Jock. He was looking around at the other men at the table now, smiling again. Jock closed his eyes and let his shoulders sag, waiting for the trembling to pass.

Capone took another swallow of wine and continued to address the men around the table. "A successful man's expected to enjoy life, right? To have his pleasures." Capone frowned a bit, not finding that last word quite what he wanted to say. "*Enthusiasms*—an eminent man is expected to have enthusiasms."

Heads nodded agreement, though no one understood what he was getting at.

"What are mine?" Capone went on. "What is that which gives me joy? Lotsa things, sure. But my favorite's baseball, like all of you know. Go to every game I can. Love it. Look at this souvenir."

Capone took a baseball bat from under the table. He held it in one fat hand, caressing it with his other. "This used to belong to the guy had the most runs-batted-in a few seasons back. This is the slugger he did it with. Ain't that a beauty?"

He got to his feet and, grasping the bat behind him

with both hands, began a slow stroll around the table. As he strolled he spoke, with his eyes half closed in thought. It sounded like some kind of rambling speech he might be practicing, to use at a gathering of the sports figures he so loved.

"Why do I love baseball? Because it teaches you about life. A man stands alone at the plate. This is the time for what? For individual achievement. There he stands—alone. But in the field, what? He's part of a team. Looks, throws, catches, hustles—part of the big team. He bats by himself the live-long day. Babe Ruth, Ty Cobb, a star like that. But if his *team don't field*—you follow me?"

Capone had reached the other end of the table. He paused briefly, looking down at Walter Payne. "Do you follow me?" he repeated.

Payne nodded uneasily, though in fact he did not. Capone smiled at him and strolled on, along the other side of the long table.

"The point is," he resumed, "all by himself what is this star? No one. Sunny day, the stands are fulla fans. What does he have to say? I'm goin' out there for myself. But *I* get nowhere unless the *whole* team's working to win!"

His ramble had brought him at last behind Jock Miller's chair. "Nobody expected that place to get raided," he said heavily. "You're right, Jock. But if there's *no* chance at all of a raid, I don't have to pay anybody to guard it!"

Capone's voice rose to a roar. "And I *was* paying guys to guard that place! And *you* didn't do what I was paying you for! *You* let me down! You *betrayed* me!"

Jock started to turn toward him, his face contorted with terror. "Al, *please*, I didn't—"

Capone brought the baseball bat over and down, smashing Jock's right shoulder.

Shrieking in agony, Jock sprawled at Capone's feet.

Right arm dangling, he tried to push himself up a little, to grasp at Capone's legs with his left hand, to plead.

Capone raised the bat high and slammed it down again, across Jock's back. The noise of breaking bones was very loud in the banquet room. Blood spattered Capone's trousers and jacket.

At the end of the table Walter Payne twisted out of his chair and went to his knees behind it, throwing up on the carpet.

But every other man around that table remained in his chair, stone-faced, watching Al Capone continue to club the corpse at his feet.

SIXTEEN

In the next two weeks Eliot's new team knocked over three more Capone establishments. Important ones. A brewery in the Stockyards District. A big still on the South Side. A warehouse in the suburb of Forest View, loaded with more imported liquor for Capone's carriage trade.

Each raid was based on leads gathered by Malone from his mysterious sources, with follow-up stakeouts to make sure they hit the right place at the right time. For carrying out the attack, Eliot reinforced his basic four-man team with as many of Lieutenant Alderson's flying squad as he thought essential. But none of them were told what was up until they reached the building to be hit. That way no member of the squad who was on the take could tip off the Capone organization in time to matter.

That they were putting a painful dent in Capone's bootleg operations was certain—especially his carriage trade. According to Malone's information, the supplies for that were running so short Capone would very soon have to import another shipment.

The day after the fourth successful raid, another front-page cartoon about Eliot Ness appeared. Same newspaper as the first one, same cartoonist.

This one had Eliot, still dressed as a crusading knight, smashing bottles of booze while Al Capone cowered in a corner tearing out his hair in frustrated fury. The caption read: "Do you mind if I break in?" The accompanying feature story was distinctly flattering.

Eliot felt somewhat uneasy about it. While it was true he was the head and driving force of the team, he knew it was James Malone who was making its attacks effective. It seemed to Eliot that Malone was doing all the leg work while he, Eliot, garnered all the publicity. But Malone liked it that way. "Let them concentrate on you," he told Eliot. "The longer I can keep operating in the shadows, the better."

The morning after the flattering cartoon appeared, Eliot entered police headquarters and was stopped by what he saw on the bulletin board near the elevator. It was the new cartoon. Under it was scrawled in red crayon, *Keep it Up!*

Obviously there were some cops around here who liked seeing Capone get hit where it hurt, even if they might still resent its taking an outsider to come in and do it for them. Eliot felt a little warmer toward the Chicago police as he climbed the stairway to his office.

Changes had been made there. A second desk, for Malone, had been installed next to his own. And a connecting storeroom had been turned into an office for Wallace and Stone. Eliot's clerk-secretary had been changed, too. The new one was one of three cops recommended and guaranteed by Malone. This one was Malone's cousin, Sean, who'd taken his retirement from the police force the previous year.

"If he's been around this long," Malone had said,

"and still can't afford a decent suit or a new car, means he's staved off temptation so far. But," Malone had added cynically, "that *could* just mean nobody's ever offered Sean a big enough bribe before. So I'll keep a close eye on him."

Sean's desk outside the office was empty when Eliot got there. And Malone wasn't inside at his desk. That didn't surprise Eliot. Malone was more often out prowling the city, tracking down new leads. As Eliot hung up his jacket, Sean came through carrying two big ledgers toward the back office.

"Where're those two from?" Eliot asked him.

"Just arrived from the Chamber of Commerce, Mr. Ness." Sean shook his head admiringly. "The way Mr. Wallace in there whips through all those big books of business records he keeps getting sure is a wonder, ain't it? Man must be a genius."

"He's an accountant," Eliot said dryly. "Stone in there too?"

"No, sir. He and Jimmy took off for somewhere real early this morning, right after I got in."

That didn't surprise Eliot, either. Increasingly, Malone was taking Stone along on his mysterious prowls.

Eliot followed Sean into the back office. Oscar Wallace was behind his desk, consulting four open ledgers that covered it and making a notation in a notebook.

"Here they are, Mr. Wallace," Sean told him.

Without looking up from his research, Wallace indicated Stone's desk. "Just leave them over there, please."

Sean placed the two new ledgers beside a stack of five already waiting on Stone's desk and went out.

Eliot looked with a small smile at the holstered revolver hanging on the wall behind Wallace, next to his riot gun. Taking part in the raids was having its effect on the dumpy accountant. He'd acquired the revolver from the headquarters arsenal, and had taken to wearing it under his jacket whenever he left the office. And just yesterday he'd come to Eliot with a suggestion about riot guns.

"I've been doing some research into it, Mr. Ness. The Winchester 97 seems to me a better riot gun for our purpose than the one we're using. I think you should look into it. A much more effective weapon."

But when not taking part in a raid, Wallace kept putting in very long hours every day, and usually late into the night, pursuing the original purpose for which he'd been sent from Washington: trying to get a clear picture of Al Capone's financial involvements.

"How are you doing, Oscar?" Eliot asked.

"It's difficult," Wallace answered, copying another item from one of the ledgers into his notebook. "Capone's organization is incredibly diverse. For example..." He turned back a page and referred to his notes there. "I have reason to believe he owns a firm calling itself Caltandar Holding Company Associations, in Toronto. Which in turn owns Green Light Laundries, Inc. ... Midwest Taxicabs ... Jolly Time Toys..."

"That reminds me," Eliot said, "I have to get a birthday present for my daughter."

"How old is she?" Wallace asked absently, concentrating on his notes.

"She'll be eight in a few days."

"Umm..." Wallace hadn't really been listening. He was turning back to another page in his notebook. "And then there's Bahama Ship-to-Shore ... Miss Lucy Togs ... Tri-County Trucking ... the list of companies is endless."

Wallace scowled at his notes. "The problem is, these businesses are all legitimate. And so far I haven't come across evidence that they're owned by Al Capone."

He sighed and looked up at Eliot finally. "*Nothing* is in his name. Legally he receives no income at all."

"Sounds to me like Capone's got himself a pretty good accountant."

"Very good. He's succeeded in creating endless financial boxes within boxes. Virtually impossible to penetrate." Wallace threw his pencil down angrily. "We *know* Capone's making millions a year from all those organization businesses—and paying no taxes. We don't have to prove all that income. If I can establish *any* payments to him at all, we can prosecute him for income tax evasion."

"Frankly," Eliot told him, "the thought of trying a murderer just for not paying his taxes doesn't exactly fill me with joy."

Wallace shrugged. "It's better than nothing."

"Maybe, but you can't even link him to any of that money."

"Not so far," Wallace admitted. He closed two of the ledgers on his desk, carried them over to Stone's desk, and brought back one of the two Sean had just delivered. Opening it, he resumed his own form of hunting.

Eliot watched him for a moment. He couldn't really believe that the way to get Capone lay in any of these ledgers. But he said, "Well, keep digging. You never know."

Sean reappeared in the connecting doorway. "Mr. Ness, you've got a visitor."

Eliot left Wallace to his work and followed Sean back into his own office.

A dapper, self-assured man in his late fifties had seated himself in the chair facing Eliot's desk. His sleek, beautifully manicured hands rested on the silver handle of an elegant walking stick. He looked up at Eliot with a smooth, ingratiating smile. "Mr. Ness?"

"Yes."

"I wonder if we could talk for a minute. I'm John O'Shea, alderman of the—"

"Yes, Alderman," Eliot interrupted, "I know who you

are. Your name has been mentioned to me by several sources."

"Ah? It's pleasant to find I'm so well known."

"Depends what you're well known for." Eliot nodded at Sean, who went out to his desk.

When he was alone with the alderman, Eliot said, "I'm rather busy right now, Mr. O'Shea. What can I do for you?"

"First of all, Mr. Ness, may I congratulate you on the startling success you've already achieved in carrying out the mission which brought you to our fair city. It is a pleasure for me to bask in your good fortune on such a lovely day."

The alderman gestured toward the office window. Eliot automatically glanced in that direction. The day outside was dim under an overcast of cloud, with a light drizzle falling. When he looked back, there was a thick envelope lying on his desk and O'Shea was smiling at him again.

Eliot pointed to the envelope. "And what have we here?"

The alderman cocked his head to one side, regarding Eliot thoughtfully for a few seconds. Then he stood up, went to the office's front door, and shut it, after which he crossed the office and shut the door to the back office. Then he came back and sat down facing Eliot across the desk again.

"Mr. Ness," he said quietly, "you're an educated man. University graduate. Studied business, I am told. So you do understand business matters."

Eliot gestured at the well-padded envelope. "And that's what this is, a business matter?"

"Let me pay you the compliment of being blunt, Mr. Ness. There is a large—a very large and very *popular* business—which your actions are causing some dismay. It would be to your advantage to cross the street, as it were, and let things take their course."

"That's as vague a 'blunt' statement as I've ever heard, Mr. O'Shea."

"Perhaps, but I believe you understand me."

"I believe I do," Eliot acknowledged. He got up, opened the door to the back office, and stepped inside.

"Mr. Wallace, would you come into the next room, please."

He waited until Wallace rose and joined him, then led the way back into his own office. The thick envelope was still on his desk, and the alderman was still seated, his smile bland.

"In Roman times," Eliot told him, "do you know what they did to a fellow who was convicted of trying to bribe a public official? They cut off his nose and sewed him in a bag with some wild animal. And then they threw the bag in the river."

He looked at Wallace and indicated the envelope on his desk. "Alderman O'Shea just offered me this envelop, Mr. Wallace. What would you suppose is inside it?"

Wallace regarded the envelope and pursed his lips. "Well, I'd say, of necessity, what is inside it is probably some worthless paper."

"Why do you suppose that?"

"Because the alderman did not make any attempt to hide it when you went to the other room to fetch me."

Eliot maintained the same politely formal tone as Wallace, as though they were discussing whether another desk could be fitted into the room without overcrowding it. "And why would Mr. O'Shea bring me an envelope stuffed with useless paper?"

"To see if you would accept or reject a bribe," Wallace answered. "This way, if your response to the bribe was negative, there'd be no evidence that he *had* attempted to offer a bribe."

"I see." Eliot picked up the envelope and ripped it

open, dumping its contents on his desk: newsprint, cut from a local newspaper.

Eliot smiled at the accountant. "You're a good detective, Mr. Wallace. Intuitive."

Wallace came close to blushing. "No intuition involved, Mr. Ness. It was a logical deduction."

Eliot turned to the alderman. "You tell your *master* that we must agree to disagree."

O'Shea was no longer smiling. He rose to his feet slowly. "I must tell you, you're making a mistake."

Eliot laughed in his face. "I've made them before. I'm beginning to enjoy it."

The alderman's veneer of well-bred coolness cracked momentarily, and his voice got a nasty rasp to it. "You fellas are *untouchable*, is that the thing? No one can get to you? Hey, *everybody* can be gotten to."

"You've done your little errand, Alderman. Now go back and tell Capone that I'll see him in Hell." Eliot strode past O'Shea and opened the door leading out to the hallway. "Now if you'll excuse us, we have work to do. I doubt that it will 'dismay' the slimy business you represent any less than our previous efforts."

But Alderman O'Shea had regained his composure. "It *has* been fascinating to make your acquaintance, sir."

He nodded politely and sauntered out, jauntily swinging his silver-headed cane.

Two nights after rejecting Alderman O'Shea's bribe offer, Eliot ran into a Capone response to that rejection when he returned home from work.

SEVENTEEN

It was two hours after dusk when Eliot pulled the Pontiac coupe to a stop in front of his house. The lights were on inside. As he climbed out of the Pontiac, carrying a gift-wrapped package, he looked toward a car standing on the other side of the street.

It was a black Cadillac touring car. The night shadows were too deep there to make out if anyone was inside it.

But Eliot automatically transferred the gift package to his left hand and unbuttoned his jacket.

A man's voice called from the Cadillac, "Good evening, Mr. Ness."

"Good evening." Eliot moved his right hand closer to the .45 holstered under his jacket.

"Hear your little girl's having her birthday tomorrow," the man in the Caddy said.

"That's right." It could be one of the neighbors, but Eliot didn't recall having seen any neighbor drive a Cadillac touring car.

He began walking across the street, ready to hurl himself down to his right if it was trouble.

But the man's voice didn't sound like trouble. It was conversational, though with a peculiar lack of any human warmth. "Nice to have a family."

"Yes, it is." Eliot was beside the Cadillac by then. There was no one inside the back of it. Only the two in front: the driver, and the man seated on Eliot's side—the one who had spoken.

Bending slightly, squinting, Eliot made out the man's face. And remembered it from photographs he'd studied. "You're Frank Nitti."

Nitti's smile was chilling. "The thing is, Mr. Ness, a man with a family should take care to see that nothing happens to them."

Eliot took a backward sidestep, very fast, and reached inside his jacket. The Cadillac shot away with its tires squealing.

Yanking out his gun, Eliot took aim through the night shadows at the car racing off. But then he held his fire. The Enforcer had been careful not to say or do anything that could justify shooting at him.

But . . .

In a sudden spasm of panic, Eliot sprinted back across the street, up onto the porch. He had the front door opened and was going through it a split-second later.

Catherine was on the sofa, flipping through a magazine, when her husband burst in. She jumped to her feet, more frightened by the expression on his face than the gun in his hand.

"Where's Cora?" he yelled.

"Up in bed. What's wrong? *Eliot?*"

He had already dropped the gift package on a chair and was racing up the stairs. Opening his daughter's door, he went in swiftly.

Cora was under the covers, sleeping peacefully.

He crouched beside the bed, listening intently, until he could hear the sound of his daughter's breathing. Then he straightened, shutting his eyes for a few seconds while he fought off a wave of dizziness.

Catherine came into Cora's doorway behind him as he backed out. "Eliot," she whispered, "what is it?"

He moved into the corridor with her, not closing Cora's door or putting his gun away or lowering his voice when he spoke. "Pack for the country. Both of you. Right now."

He ran down the stairs to his study. Catherine hurried down after him. When she entered the study he was taking a shotgun and a box of shells out of the closet there.

"Eliot, will you please tell me—"

"Everything's going to be fine," he told her, but his voice was shaking. "You just pack. And get Cora up and dressed, ready to get out of here. Quickly—*please*."

He put the .45 pistol on his desk and began loading the shotgun. Catherine turned and hurried back upstairs.

Laying the loaded shotgun across his desk next to the pistol, Eliot snatched up his phone and put a call through to Malone's house. There was no answer. He tried his office next, on the chance Malone had gone back there.

The one who answered was Oscar Wallace, still there working on his ledgers.

"Malone around?" Eliot asked him.

"No."

"Well where the hell is he?"

"I don't know. He called in about an hour ago and said he'd be coming in but he didn't say when."

"What about Stone?"

"Not here either." By then Wallace had caught the urgency in Eliot's voice. "What's the matter?"

Eliot told him.

* * *

When a Ford sedan turned into the street and pulled in to the curb in front of the house, Eliot stepped out onto the porch holding his shotgun ready.

But it was Oscar Wallace who climbed out of the Ford, followed by Malone's cousin, Sean. Eliot lowered the shotgun a bit and went down the steps to them.

"I left a message on Malone's desk," Wallace told him, "so if he gets back before—"

But Eliot was already speaking to Sean. "You got anything with you besides that pistol you're wearing?"

"Got a sawed-off in the car," Sean said.

"Good. Now, there's a place in the country where my wife and I took our daughter for a picnic last Sunday. There's a house near there takes in paying guests. My wife'll show you the way. Drive them there and take a room next to the one they rent. Stick by them day and night. I'll get you help when I can. And don't make any calls telling *anybody* where they are."

"Okay, Mr. Ness, no problem."

Eliot turned and called toward the house, "All right, let's go."

Catherine came out of the house holding their daughter by the hand.

"I'll bring the bags out," Eliot said as they came down from the porch.

"Want some help with those bags?" Sean asked him.

"No, stay put here and keep your eye on the street." Eliot handed Wallace his shotgun and hurried into the house as his wife and child got into the back seat of the Ford.

He came out quickly, carrying the suitcases Catherine had packed. Wallace stood on the sidewalk watching the street in one direction, Sean watching the other. Eliot put the suitcases in the Ford's trunk and went around to the rear seat of the car, bending to look in at his wife and child.

"Daddy," Cora asked, "how long are we going to be away for?"

"Just a little while, honey."

"Will you come and be with us?"

"As soon as I can," he assured her, and straightened to tell Sean, "Drive north up the street. My wife'll tell you where to turn off and give you the directions to take the rest of the way."

"Yes, sir."

"Anything happens—anybody *looks* like they're coming at my family, *you shoot first*. You understand?"

"Don't worry, Mr. Ness, I'll take care of 'em. Jimmy'd kill me if I let you down."

"Daddy," Cora called, "you're going to miss my birthday tomorrow."

"Yes, honey, I am, but I'll make it up to you next year." Eliot suddenly remembered. "Wait. Hold it a minute."

He ran back into the house and came out with the gift-wrapped package. Leaning into the rear of the Ford, he handed it to his wife and told Cora, "Your birthday present. Mommy'll give it to you tomorrow morning."

He kissed his daughter, then his wife.

"You take care of yourself," Catherine whispered.

"Oh, I'm going to." Eliot straightened, shut the rear door, and told Sean, "Now, *go*."

Sean got in behind the wheel and started the Ford. Eliot took his shotgun back from Wallace as the Ford headed north up the street. The two of them stood together looking after it.

There was the noise of screeching tires as a car came racing around the corner behind them. Both of them spun toward it, Wallace yanking the revolver out from under his jacket and Eliot leveling the shotgun.

The car jolted to a halt well before reaching them. The driver jumped out. It was Malone, hands held high, signaling "Don't shoot." He reached inside the car, pulled out a submachine gun fitted with a drum ammunition magazine built to hold fifty rounds. He came jogging down the street to them carrying it.

"Your wife and kid . . .?" he asked Eliot anxiously.

It was Wallace who answered. "They're fine. Just took off for the country with your cousin."

Malone relaxed, lowering his tommy gun. "Well, that's all right, then. Good idea, getting them out've the way for a while."

Eliot told him, "I came home and there were two of them, in a car across the street there."

"Sure they were Capone hoods?" Malone asked him.

"No question. One of them was Frank Nitti."

Malone's mouth tightened. "*That* vicious bastard."

"If I hadn't gotten here when I did, they could have gone in my house and—"

"No," Malone said. "They weren't here to *do* anything. If they were you wouldn't't've found your house in one piece. I forgot to tell you. There's one other step Capone'll sometimes try, between bribing you and killing. *Scaring* you out."

"I *am* scared," Eliot told him. "And *mad*. And I want to scare Capone. I want to do *worse* than that. I want to *hurt* that man, Malone. Hurt him worse than he's ever been hurt before."

Malone was smiling thinly. "Well, then, Merry Christmas. Because we've got some news."

Another car turned into the street and slowed to a stop beside them. Stone jumped out looking brimful of barely contained excitement.

Malone nodded at him. "Tell 'em Guiseppe."

Stone told it, his voice hushed in awe. "There's gonna be a huge convoy of imported liquor slipping through the border from Canada tomorrow for Capone!"

"We got the time and the place," Malone said. "The whole thing."

"How'd you come by this information?" Eliot asked him.

"Second rule of police work," Malone told him phlegmatically. "The best way to keep a secret source secret is don't tell the boss."

EIGHTEEN

The rugged, uninhabited terrain surrounding them was covered with snow that glistened in the sunlight. But that sun did little to warm the frigid air, and dark clouds were beginning to roll in from farther north, moving low over the sharp peaks of the highest hills.

Twisting its way between the bottoms of the steep slopes was a dirt road. It had been iced over for the past two months, and there was no sign any vehicles had attempted to travel it during that time. It was not a road any driver would care to attempt in the wintertime, unless a strong reason for wanting to slip across the border undetected compensated for the difficulty through this seldom-patrolled area.

The road led to a short, narrow bridge spanning a mountain stream that pounded its way through fallen rocks. The bridge, and the land on this side of it, belonged to the United States. At the other end of the bridge was Canada.

Eliot Ness stood on the crest of a rocky slope overlooking the iced-over dirt road at this end of the bridge. Like the men he'd brought with him, he wore a sheepskin coat and a hat with padded earflaps to combat the intense cold. The man he was speaking with was Captain Ardley of the Royal Canadian Mounted Police.

"There'll be five big trucks," he told the Mountie captain, "coming down out of your country loaded with very expensive liquor. According to our information, some high-level executive of the Capone organization will be coming up by car to meet that liquor convoy. Bound to be accompanied by other cars carrying Capone gunmen."

"You don't have the name of this Capone executive?" Captain Ardley asked him.

"No, that we don't know. I do know he'll be carrying full payment for this shipment in cash. Almost certainly he'll cross the border and deliver it on your side to a representative of the Canadian firm supplying the liquor. That representative is a legitimate businessman as long as he operates in your country. He wouldn't come over here, where accepting payments for liquor would be a criminal offense."

"You won't seize the Capone executive on this side, while he still has that money on him?"

"No. Let him go over and deliver it, and come back with the trucks." Eliot's eyes got a faint gleam of malicious pleasure. "All that cash will be lost to Capone, anyway. Along with everything else I intend to take from him. The Canadian firm fulfills its obligation when it turns over the shipment to Capone's executive. No way Capone can get his money back after that."

Eliot had phoned Mountie headquarters before flying out of Chicago, to arrange for whatever cooperation could be given. That cooperation was painfully limited, as Captain Ardley made clear.

"I have ten of my men hidden in the woods on the other side of that bridge, Mr. Ness. But you do realize there's no law against transporting alcoholic beverages in my country. So I can't arrest the men in those trucks over there. And I obviously can't come over to this side to help you enforce the laws of your country."

"I do realize that," Eliot said. That didn't make it any less unpleasant. His own force was certain to be outnumbered by the Capone gunmen.

"I could," the Mountie captain suggested, "stop the trucks on my side and do a weapons search. If the men with those trucks are armed, that *would* be a violation of law and I could arrest them."

"They won't be armed, not on your side of the line. As you point out, they're not breaking any laws there by moving liquor. Why would they risk getting arrested for carrying guns? No, the guns will be brought by the hoods that come up through here to meet the convoy and take it to Chicago."

"Another possibility," Captain Ardley said. "I can turn them back at the frontier, since they won't have an import license from your government."

Eliot shook his head. "They'd just come back through in a few days, some other route. No, let them through. I want them on this side, where I can confiscate all that Capone liquor and arrest all his men that're with it."

Captain Ardley made a rueful face. "I'm afraid I'm not being much help."

"You can do one thing for me," Eliot told him. "After we hit the convoy on this side, block your end of the bridge, and stop any of them that try to escape back that way."

"Glad to oblige. Once you've let them know they're under arrest I've every right—even obligation—to prevent fugitives from fleeing your country into mine."

"Thanks, Captain. That will help."

"You'll have the element of surprise on your side, too, Mr. Ness. They won't be expecting your attack here. And surprise, as we both know, is half the battle."

Later Eliot regretted it and blamed it on the strain of anticipating that battle, but for a brief moment his irritation broke through. "*Surprise* is half the battle," he mimicked angrily. "Many things are half the battle, dammit! *Losing's* the other half of the battle."

He stopped himself abruptly. "Sorry, Captain. I could use a better grip on my nerves, it seems."

Captain Ardley smiled. "Quite understandable. No offense taken, and no apology required. Good luck to you, Mr. Ness."

Eliot watched him climb down the slope to the road. The Mountie captain headed for the Canadian end of the bridge. Eliot turned away and crossed the ridge behind him to the slope that led down the other side of the hill.

Just under the ridge Malone and Wallace were opening a large packing case they'd brought along with them. Eliot looked below them toward the route by which Stone and the other three men would soon be joining them.

The other three men were members of the flying squad. Malone and Stone had picked them up from their homes—without prior warning by phone. They hadn't been given any explanation at all until they were on their way inside the Ford Tri-Motor that flew them from Chicago. And the remote strip where the plane landed, eight miles from this point, had no telephone contact with the outside world.

Another thing that landing strip didn't have was any form of land transportation available, other than a single ancient taxicab which was not big enough for all of them. It had made the first trip carrying Eliot, Malone, and Wallace, together with the packing crate. Then it had gone back to fetch the others.

Eliot turned to watch Malone take one of the submachine guns out of the crate and swiftly assemble it.

"One tommy gun for each of us," Malone said to Wallace, "to equalize what we may lack in manpower. Popu-

larly known these days as a Chicago piano." He got a
drum magazine from the crate, adding cheerily, "Fifty
rounds per. Load on Sunday and shoot all week!"

He showed Wallace how to attach the drum to the
tommy gun. "Now you're the only one of us never handled one of these, so pay attention. This baby fires eight
hundred rounds a minute, but the magazine only holds
fifty. So you don't just squeeze the trigger and hang on.
Short bursts. And when your drum runs dry you can slap
in a fresh one in five seconds if—"

"It's too late to start teaching him," Eliot cut in. "He
can't learn without a lot of practice shooting, and that
convoy could be waiting just the other side of that
stream by now, close enough to hear it."

Wallace hefted his riot gun. "I'd rather stick to what I
already know, anyway."

Malone considered, and nodded. "Okay. But here's a
couple other equalizers you do know how to handle." He
reached deep in the crate and brought out two hand grenades. "Two for each of us," he said.

Wallace hesitated. "I don't know."

"You do know how to throw a ball, don't you?"

"Well, yes, but—"

"You throw this the same way. Just pull this pin here
first. Then throw it fast, before it explodes."

"I don't think I'll need—"

"Better to have it and not need it," Malone told him
flatly, "than to need it and not have it."

Oscar Wallace accepted the grenades reluctantly,
being very careful when he stuck them in his coat
pockets.

The sound of an approaching car drew their attention
to the route from the airstrip. The old taxicab came to a
stop where the path ran out down there. Stone and the
three members of the flying squad got out. One of them
was Sergeant McGough, the one who'd led Squad B during Eliot's first, disastrous warehouse raid.

Watching Stone lead the way up the slope, Eliot muttered, "I hope those three do what's needed today."

"They will," Malone said.

"Any of them could be a Capone spy."

"Makes no difference," Malone said. "A cop on the take might tip off the guy that's paying him, or conceal evidence for him, or look the other way. But in a fight alongside other cops, he'll do what he's supposed to. Cop pride. Crazy, maybe, but a fellow's got to be crazy in the first place to wanta be a cop."

NINETEEN

The seven of them waited on the hill, hidden in deep shadow between two looming boulders, watching the road below where it reached to the U.S. end of the bridge.

Malone, Wallace, and Stone stood to one side of Eliot. Sergeant McGough and the other two from the flying squad stood on his other side, each clutching a weapon and coping with the approaching confrontation in his own way.

The sky had become overcast. A light drizzle fell from it, and the wind had acquired a sharp bite.

Oscar Wallace tucked his riot gun under one arm and took off his bifocals, using his thumb to wipe the mist off them.

Eliot checked his watch, though the clock in his head told him there was still considerable waiting ahead. He felt an edgy need to make sure.

"Take it easy," Malone told him. "It'll happen—in time. That's what the job is: waiting. But don't wait for it to happen, don't even want it to happen. Wait like you and the clock are stopped. Limbo. You start up again when it *does* happen, with your attention spread to take in everything at the same time. All points of the compass."

"What are you, my tutor?"

"Yes, sir, that I am."

On the other side of Eliot, Sergeant McGough shifted his tommy gun to his left hand, drew his revolver, and started to check it.

Malone looked past Eliot at him. "Didn't you already check that five minutes ago?"

McGough looked embarrassed. "Guess I did."

"Then leave it alone. You're a good cop, Sergeant. You did good on those raids. You're gonna do just fine this time."

Eliot looked at the rock formations jutting out of the slope below, and those in the slope that rose from the other side of the road. He raised his voice to include all the men to either side of him. "When we move down, keep to the cover of those rocks as much as possible. But remember, they can cover the opposition, too. So don't get careless moving past any of them."

"And the Devil's waitin' in Hell for him that's not careful *enough*," Malone chimed in with a semblance of a grin.

"You know what, Malone," Stone told him, "you look even meaner when you smile than when you don't."

But his teeth were chattering, breaking up some of the words.

Malone gave him a concerned squint. "Scared, Giuseppe?"

"Just awful cold."

"Stamp your feet awhile. That'll keep you warm." Malone glanced at Eliot and shrugged. "You learn *something* walking a beat twenty years." He scowled to himself and added softly: "Mostly about snitches and standing in the rain."

The cold drizzle ended. The clouds began to break up, letting sunlight stream through again.

Stone abruptly ceased stamping his feet and raised a hand for silence, listening.

Eliot eased forward a couple of inches and looked down—not toward the bridge but in the opposite direction: to where the road first curved into view around the projecting side of a cliff to the south.

Seconds later a large black touring car came around that bend. Another came around after it, close behind. The two heavy cars approached the bridge slowly, the snow chains on their tires making crackling noises in the iced road.

They came to a halt near the bridge, almost directly below the seven men on the crest above, pulling over as far to one side of the road as possible. Men climbed out. Some carried rifles, others shotguns, two had submachine guns. All would have handguns as well. They spread out, looking up both slopes.

Eliot moved back a few inches, though he knew the men below couldn't see him and his group, shrouded in shadow between the boulders. He counted: four gunmen from each car; and the drivers still inside would be armed, too. That made ten of them—so far.

When the gunmen spotted nothing to worry them, two walked across the short bridge to the road on the Canadian side. Satisfied with their surveillance there, they recrossed the bridge and joined the others around the big touring cars. Then the Capone gorillas just stood there, waiting.

Eliot told his men softly, "Don't move until I do. Don't fire unless I give the order—or if they start shooting first."

"Oh, they will," Malone whispered. "Don't even

dream they won't. And when you fire back, hold low and squeeze and put your man down—for good—'cause that's what he'll be trying to do to you. Shoot to *kill*."

He turned to Oscar Wallace, who was hastily wiping his bifocals clean again. "Did you hear what I said?"

"Yessir, I did," Wallace whispered. "Shoot to kill." He slipped his glasses back on and gripped his riot gun with both hands.

A new sound reached Eliot. He watched and waited.

A sleek limousine appeared around the cliff side to the south. One of the gunmen below Eliot raised an arm and signaled to it. Moving as slowly as the previous pair of cars, the limousine came on toward them and the bridge.

When it reached the parked touring cars the limousine slowed even more and began to ease past them. There was just barely enough room for it to do so.

It was going to be impossible, when the trucks came across, for them to get by. The cars would have to lead the way south, with the truck convoy following, until they got to some wider stretch of road. But Eliot didn't intend to let any of that happen.

He turned his head and whispered to Malone, Wallace, and Stone, "If it comes to shooting, knock out those two touring cars first. Their tires, engine—I want them immobilized, so the trucks can't get by. The Mounties'll block them from backing out the other way."

The limousine stopped after passing the second touring car. The gunman who'd signaled to it bent down to speak to someone in back.

Eliot raised binoculars to his eyes and trained them on the limousine. In the front seat were the driver and another man, powerfully built, a typical bodyguard type. Eliot shifted focus to the rear seat.

There was only one man in the back. A short man wearing a raccoon coat and a fur hat tugged down to protect his ears. He had glasses and a thick mustache.

His gloved hands held a briefcase with a combination lock on his lap.

The gunman speaking to him pulled back and straightened up. The limousine moved forward again, onto the bridge. It crossed it and was lost to sight around a tight curve in the forest-flanked road on the other side.

Eliot lowered his binoculars. He didn't know the man in the back seat of the limousine was named Walter Payne, but he did know that man had to be the "high-level executive" from Al Capone's organization.

"If the truck convoy sticks to previous procedure," he told his group, keeping his voice very low, "each truck will be carrying two men up front, the driver and a guard. But it's unlikely they'll be coming out of Canada carrying weapons on them. I think they'll be expecting to pick up guns from those two cars down there. Or else get them out of hiding places in the back of their trucks once they cross the border here."

Eliot turned to the three men from the flying squad. "I want you three to concentrate on those trucks. Cut the men in them off from the cars—and shoot any trying to go around the trucks to open their back doors."

McGough and the other two nodded.

Eliot looked into the eyes of each of them in turn. "You're responsible for keeping those men from getting arms and joining in the fight. Don't let us down."

They understood the implication. Their faces hardened, and they looked at each other searchingly. Then they looked at Eliot again. They didn't nod again—just met his steady gaze.

Fifteen minutes later the limousine came back across the bridge. It stopped when it reached the gunmen standing around the two touring cars. The bodyguard got out of the front seat and stood there looking back toward the bridge while he lit a cigarette. The limousine's driver remained inside at the wheel. The man in the raccoon coat stayed in the back seat.

The liquor trucks emerged out of the woods on the Canadian side and began rumbling slowly across the narrow bridge—five of them, close behind each other.

Eliot tipped the muzzle of his submachine gun at the sky, took a deep breath, and let it out slowly. The first burst would be to let the Capone mob down there know he meant business—and to signal Captain Ardley to seal off retreat into Canada with his Mounties.

The lead truck neared the cars blocking the road and stopped, as the fifth and last truck came onto the bridge —bringing all of them onto U.S. territory. Eliot slid his finger across the tommy gun's trigger. Down beside the limousine, the bodyguard flipped his cigarette away and got back in the front seat next to the driver.

Eliot triggered off a three-shot burst that echoed loudly among the surrounding mountainsides.

"Federal officers!" he yelled. "You're under arrest! Lay down your arms and—"

The rest of it got lost in the barrage of gunfire that exploded as the Capone gorillas on the road began shooting at the sound of his voice while they darted for cover behind cars and rock formations along the base of the opposite slope.

Eliot's men went into action in almost the same instant.

TWENTY

"Well, hell," Malone said to himself, "you got to die of *something*."

And then he was moving down the slope through the enemy gunfire, spraying one of the black touring cars with his tommy gun, his bullets punching gaping holes through its hood.

Stone started running down a moment later, shooting at the second touring car—with Oscar Wallace scrambling after him, desperately trying to catch up.

Sergeant McGough and his two from the flying squad were angling away swiftly in the direction of the truck convoy.

Eliot headed down toward the limousine. The man in its back seat was the one he wanted most. That high-level Capone executive. And he wanted the man alive—to see if he could be squeezed into spilling his guts.

By then everything was happening at once.

The Capone gunmen were firing from behind cars and rocks at the four men of the federal attack team, who darted from one bit of cover to another as they closed the distance.

The truck convoy had come to a halt when the gunfight broke out. Two men jumped down from the first two trucks and started toward the cars. Submachine-gun bursts from the three flying squad officers drove them back behind the protection of the trucks.

Men jumped from the third and fourth trucks and ran back along the bridge to escape to the Canadian side of the border. The driver of the last truck started to back up with the same idea.

A team of Mounties appeared on the road at the Canadian end of the bridge, firing warning shots into the air, sealing off that line of retreat.

One of the truck drivers climbed over the side of the bridge, aiming to get away underneath it. Bursts from the flying squad trio ripped him loose and dropped his lifeless body into the rapids of the torrential stream below.

The limousine with the Capone executive in it was easing forward now, swinging to get around the two touring cars, both of which had become as immobilized as Eliot had wanted. Their engines had been transformed into junk by the bullets thudding into them.

Eliot went to one knee to steady his aim and swung his submachine gun in a low, tight arc, triggering a long burst at the limousine's wheels. The limousine slewed to a skittering halt as both tires on Eliot's side burst to shreds.

The doors on the other side were thrown open. The executive in the raccoon coat jumped out of the back and began climbing away along the slope there, lugging his briefcase. The bodyguard came out of the front seat and followed, protecting his back. Eliot ran down to cross the road after them.

The bodyguard glanced back and saw him coming. He turned fully, bringing his revolver around to shoot. A burst from Eliot's tommy gun shattered his right leg. The bodyguard went down in an ungainly heap and stayed that way, out cold from shock.

In that instant the driver popped up inside the limousine and leveled a shotgun through its open window. Eliot dove to his right, as fast and as far as he could. The shotgun boomed.

Pellets from its spreading load tore at the back of his sheepskin coat as he hit the ground and did a fast roll. A second blast from the shotgun chopped up gouts of snow, ice, and frozen mud less than two feet from his face. Eliot rolled up on one hip and squeezed his trigger. Nothing happened. The tommy gun had jammed. He dropped it and clawed for the .45 automatic under his coat, knowing he didn't have enough time left.

Something that looked like a ball fell out of the sky and bounced in the road beside the limousine. It didn't bounce like a ball would. In mid-bounce the grenade exploded. The shotgun clattered on the road ten feet away from the limousine. What was left of the driver's head and arms hung down the outside of the limousine's door.

Eliot looked for the source of the grenade and saw Malone up among the rock formations of the opposite slope. He only saw him for a second. The next second Malone was gone among the rocks, hunting for other matters that needed to be dealt with.

Higher along that same slope, off to the right, the fleeing Capone executive in the raccoon coat was still climbing. Eliot spotted a second Capone man not far below the first one, going in the same direction. Shoving to his feet, Eliot tugged out his handgun and crossed the road to climb that slope.

Behind him and some fifteen yards to the left along the road, Stone was trying to maneuver around one of the wrecked touring cars to get at gunmen barricaded there. He was almost in position when a hood crouched behind the second car suddenly straightened and fired at him over its roof.

Stone's head was punched violently backward and his brain seemed to explode, sending him reeling. "Oh, my God," he gasped as the ground came up and hit him. He repeated it silently in Italian as darkness engulfed him.

The hood leaned around the back of the car, taking aim to make sure Stone was finished with a second shot.

Oscar Wallace jumped over Stone's motionless figure with his riot gun thundering point-blank. The hood was blown away, his chest caved in. Swinging to fire at another dodging between rocks at the base of the slope, Wallace found he'd used up his last shot. And at that moment an enemy machine gunner came around the front of the second touring car.

Wallace swung the riot gun like a club, slugging the man across the temple. The clubbed man fell over the car's bullet-ripped fender and rolled off it, sprawling unconscious across the road.

Crouching beside Stone, Wallace yanked his revolver from its holster and took aim at a figure approaching out of the rocks. He stopped himself from shooting just in time. The approaching figure was Malone, coming to help with Stone.

The man in the raccoon coat had vanished.

Eliot came to a stop halfway up the slope, carefully scanning the scattered pine trees and rock formations around him. But he couldn't locate his quarry. He kept looking.

Above him, near the top of the slope, there was a movement behind a small clump of evergreen bushes. A figure emerged. But not the one in the raccoon coat. This was the other Capone man Eliot had seen making the same climb.

The man up there spotted Eliot below at the same time. He raised a fist that held a pistol. But then he lowered it again. The distance was too great for either of them to do any accurate shooting with a handgun. Eliot watched the gunman hurry away, over the crest, and disappear behind it.

Going after the one in the raccoon coat?

Eliot scanned the slope again. Seeing no one else to follow, he went on up, holding his automatic ready and climbing fast.

When he topped the rise he stopped against the protection of a thick pine tree and looked at what was down below the other side of the hill—an old cabin with a sagging roof. Maybe some trapper's shack, long abandoned. It was three-sided, built against the base of a low cliff. From his vantage point Eliot could see only one of the three sides. It had a door, sagging slightly open.

He studied the surrounding land. The gunman wasn't in sight. Neither was the man in the raccoon coat. Either or both of them could be inside that cabin, waiting for him to show himself close enough to be shot down.

Eliot circled down, following routes that kept him to the cover of rocks, trees, bushes. The second side of the cabin had a window. No glass in it, but half a warped shutter. The other half lay on the ground below the window, almost covered by snow.

He circled further until he could see the third side of the cabin—the back, if the one with the door was the front. The back had no door or window. Much of the wall there had collapsed, leaving a large opening. But he couldn't see anything inside that opening, only deep shadows.

Eliot circled back to the side of the cabin that had the window and crouched behind a stand of frozen bushes. That put him within easy handgun range of the cabin. He couldn't get any closer without stepping into the open and exposing himself as a perfect target.

After considering the position for a few seconds, he shifted the .45 automatic to his left hand and reached into his coat pocket with his right. He took out a grenade.

Pulling the pin with his teeth, Eliot lobbed it high over the cabin. It was a long time since he'd played sandlot ball, but his aim was accurate. The grenade landed exactly where he'd wanted it to: in front of the partially opened door.

The force of the grenade's detonation blasted the sagging door inward off its last hinge.

A split second later the gunman came darting out of the cabin in the opposite direction: through the opening in the back wall. If the explosion had stunned him, it hadn't slowed his reflexes any. He had the pistol in his right fist ready to fire as he did a fast turn to locate Eliot.

"Throw it down!" Eliot yelled. "You're covered!"

Instead the gunman spun toward the sound of his voice and fired twice so fast the shots blended together —and with incredible accuracy.

One of the slugs cut through the frozen bushes and missed Eliot's head by a scant inch. He didn't realize he was shooting back until he felt the recoil against the heel of his hand.

The bullet got the gunman in the stomach. He sagged, his knees bending, his left hand clutching at the wound. But he didn't go down or drop his gun. Instead he came staggering around the back corner of the cabin toward Eliot.

He tripped over his feet and went to his knees, the pistol lowering until it touched the ground, still gripped by his right hand. His bloody left hand jerked away from his wound and joined his right hand in trying to lift the pistol.

Eliot stood up and stepped out of the bushes, shouting, "Don't be a damn fool! Drop it!"

But the pistol kept coming up. When he could see its muzzle pointing at him Eliot fired again. The shot hammered the gunman's chest, smashing through his ribs and into his heart. He tipped backward against the bottom of the cabin's side wall and then settled into the snow there.

Eliot walked over and looked down at the dead gunman, hearing himself snarl at him, "I *warned* you! Didn't you hear what I said? Are you *deaf*? Crazy? You thug, are you finished playing your games? Are you *done*?"

He stopped himself with a violent effort, feeling dazed, his insides churning. He turned and put his back to the side wall, leaning against it, listening.

The sound of gunfire on the other side of the hill, down at the bridge and road, had ended. There was only silence now. Eliot fumbled in his pocket and got out a cigarette. Then he saw Malone coming out of the woods toward him.

He stuck the cigarette between his teeth and searched his pockets for matches as Malone reached him.

"Saw you head over this way," Malone said, "and thought I'd better come see if you needed help." He looked down at the dead hood. "Seems like you don't."

"I *had* to kill him," Eliot said, finding he was still having difficulty with his breathing.

Malone nodded, studying the inert gunman in the snow. "Yeah, dead as Julius Caesar."

"I've never . . . killed anyone before."

Malone regarded Eliot's face. "Well, would you rather it was *you* layin' there?"

Eliot steadied himself. "No, I would not."

"Then you did your duty. Go home and sleep well tonight. First rule of law enforcement, remember?"

Eliot lit his cigarette. "Any of ours hit?"

"Giuseppe took a head wound, but he'll be all right. Just a crease—left him a little concussed. Boy's got a hard, thick skull. Another essential for a good cop."

"Anybody else?"

"McGough got shot through both legs. But no bones broke. Mountie medic's taking care of him and Giuseppe."

"What about the Capone mob?"

"Couple got away—I think only two. The rest—them that ain't dead—are prisoners, handcuffed nice and tidy."

"Who's guarding them?"

"The other two flying squad boys." Malone registered Eliot's sudden tension and shook his head. "Don't worry, they ain't gonna let any prisoner escape. Not even if they'd want to. Not with all those Mounties standing around looking at them admiringly."

Malone tapped Eliot on the chest with a finger. "Wake up, boyo, we did it. Got all that Capone liquor, his trucks, his men . . ."

"Not all of his men," Eliot murmured, thinking of the one he'd lost—the Capone executive in the raccoon coat.

Pushing away from the side wall, he started around the front of the cabin. It was time to go back over the rise and down to the bridge road. But when he was near the cabin door what he saw up on the rise stopped him.

There were three men coming down toward him.

Malone came up beside him and said delightedly, "Well, lookee what we got here."

Two of the approaching men were Oscar Wallace and Captain Ardley. Wallace was carrying a locked briefcase.

Between Wallace and the Mountie captain, handcuffed, was the man in the raccoon coat.

TWENTY-ONE

Wallace indicated the handcuffed man between him and the Mountie officer as they reached Eliot and Malone in front of the cabin. "He tried to escape across the stream into Canada. Captain Ardley kindly turned him back to me, as a fugitive from U.S. justice. According to his wallet his name's Walter Payne. Which means—"

But Malone finished it for him, nodding happily. "Which means what we got here's Al Capone's head bookkeeper. Lovely."

Eliot began to smile, too. "Well, well—that makes him an even better catch than I was hoping for." He gestured formally to the blown-open cabin door. "Won't you step into my parlor, Mr. Payne? For a little conversation."

Malone grabbed Walter Payne's thin arm and dragged him inside. The others followed. There was no furniture at all left in the cabin. Malone shoved Payne to the floor in a corner. "Well, Payne," he said softly, "you've come a long way up from Colosimo's Cafe, haven't you. And now you're about to go a long way *down*. The things that can happen to you, when you decide to take a little vacation in the north woods—and wind up opening a shooting gallery."

Eliot and Captain Ardley joined Malone, standing and looking down at the little bookkeeper. Oscar Wallace settled on the floor near them with Payne's briefcase on his lap, fiddling with its lock. Payne didn't look at any of them. He sat with his manacled wrists on his raised knees, staring blankly through his thick lenses at the opposite wall, the weak chin under his thick mustache as stubborn as it could manage to look.

Eliot took out a notebook and pen and told him, "I want you to write down the names of your fellow executives in the Capone organization. I want you to write down the names of your government contacts."

Payne didn't respond in any way, as though he couldn't even hear the demand.

"Perhaps you don't understand just how much trouble it is you've gotten yourself into," Eliot snapped. "You've fired on federal law enforcement officers."

"I did *not*," Payne said through clenched teeth. "I didn't even have a gun. I never do."

"You did this time," Malone lied blandly. "I saw you using it. I saw you shoot Officer Stone in the head."

"That's not true!" Payne blurted. "That . . . you're . . ."

Malone cut him short. "You're just lucky Stone's not dead. But it's bad enough. For you, Payne. Taking part in an armed attempt to resist arrest. Wounding an officer in pursuance of his duty. . ."

"You can cooperate with us," Eliot told Payne harshly, "or you can be tough in Leavenworth for the next thirty years. Is that what you want?"

Malone beamed at Capone's bookkeeper. "You're going in for all *day*, baby."

Oscar Wallace looked up from the briefcase. "I can't

get this lock open. Mr. Payne refused to tell me the combination."

"Lean back a second, Oscar," Malone said, turning toward him and drawing his gun.

Wallace backed away from the briefcase hastily. Malone shot the lock apart, the blast bringing a shower of dust cascading down on them from the sagging roof.

Wallace picked up the briefcase, opened it wide, and investigated its contents. Taking out a couple of small ledgers, he leafed through one of them with sharpening interest. "What can it be that we have *here*?"

He handed the ledger up to Eliot, who began turning its pages, studying what Payne had jotted on them. The first page had the word "Disbursements." After that each page had a different heading at the top, in some kind of code he couldn't translate. Under the heading on each page were three lists, side by side. The first two lists were also coded. The third was a list of dates.

Eliot looked from the ledger to Wallace. "What is this?" he asked, though he already had a strong notion.

"I've seen hundreds like it in my experience as an accountant," Wallace said. "It must be what it says on the first page: money paid out. By the Capone organization, in this case, since this gentleman turns out to be its bookkeeper. The coded heading at the top of each page would represent a particular area or business firm or non-business occupation group."

"Police precincts, for example," Eliot said. "Prohibition agents...wards...circuit courts...political parties."

"It would seem likely, in this case," Wallace acknowledged. "And these lists on each page—the first two would be the names of the individual recipients of the payments and the amounts they received, in code, next to the dates they were paid."

Eliot turned back to Walter Payne. "*Bribes*, that's

what these are, right? Lists of bribes, who they went to, how much, and when."

Payne fought down panic. "It's nothing, and there's nothing you can make out of it."

Wallace, who had been leafing through the other ledger, said excitedly, "This one's even more interesting."

Eliot dropped the first ledger in Wallace's lap and took the second one, looking through it swiftly. The pages in this one had headings that read "Dispensation," "Delivery," "Payments." Each page had more lists in code, followed by dates.

"Is this what I think it is?" Eliot asked Wallace.

Wallace nodded. "Must be. Goods delivered and sums of money *received* by the Capone organization. And if we can establish that any of these coded entries represent income to Al Capone, then we can put Capone away."

Eliot brandished the second ledger at Walter Payne. "I want you to tell us which of these codes stand for Al Capone."

Payne maintained a blank-faced silence.

Malone stabbed a finger at him. "You're going to do the whole thing in the joint, baby, lest you help us here."

"It's your only hope of obtaining leniency, Payne," Eliot told him firmly. "You're going to translate all these entries for us."

"In *Hell*," Payne whispered, with a flare of open defiance.

"In Hell?" Malone snarled. "This ain't the First Ward, Payne. You're muckin' with the *feds* here, pal— the *G*. And you're going to hang higher'n Hayman unless you cooperate."

Payne forced a bored expression. "Don't be childish. I don't intend to say anything without my attorneys present."

Wallace looked unhappily at Eliot. "This man can

finger Al Capone for us. This man can put Al Capone behind bars."

Malone nodded to himself and bent down to Payne. "Mister *hardcase*... Figure you can just wait until Capone sends some fancy lawyers to get you out've this one? Well not with *me*."

Abruptly, so fast none of the others saw it coming, Malone slapped Payne very hard.

The force of it twisted Payne face down on the floor, knocking his glasses askew. A thin sound of shocked pain bubbled out of him. He pressed a hand to his hurt cheek, fumbled his glasses back in position.

Captain Ardley had taken a step backward, his face frozen in an expression of distaste.

Malone seized a handful of Payne's coat and yanked him back up to a sitting position. "We got to have that information, Payne, I am *not* fuckin' with you!" He raised his hand to slap him again.

Eliot glanced at the Mountie captain and snapped, "No, Malone, not that way."

"The *hell* you say." Malone's face was darkening with rage now, his eyes burning into Payne's. "You're gonna talk, pal. You're gonna *beg* to talk."

Payne cringed away from him, but desperately clung to silence.

Malone straightened in frustration. "*Somebody's* going to talk!" He twisted around and snatched the ledger from Eliot. "That other gorilla we left handcuffed outside..." He stalked out of the cabin before Eliot could grasp what he was getting at.

Going around the side of the cabin, Malone crouched over the gunman Eliot had killed. From the direction down which Payne had been brought to the cabin, he couldn't have seen the corpse here. Malone stuck the ledger in his pocket and took out a pair of handcuffs, locking one bracelet around one of the dead man's wrists.

"Hey, *you*," he yelled as he did so, "on your feet! I need you to translate this book! And you're going to!"

Gripping the front of the dead gunman's coat, Malone lifted the body from the ground and dragged it back around the front corner of the cabin. Stopping just short of the cabin door, he shouted, "Start with this page! What's it mean, this code word here? Who's it stand for?"

It was loud enough to be heard clearly by everyone inside the cabin. And what they heard was the voice of a man gone berserk, utterly out of control.

"I won't ask you again!" Malone snarled. He closed one hand around the throat of the dead man, just under the chin, and propped the body up with it. His other hand drew his gun and stuck it in the dead man's mouth. "What's the matter, can't talk with a gun in your mouth? Too late anyway. I *told* you I wouldn't ask twice!"

Malone fired the gun—and heaved the body in through the open doorway.

He handled the throw just right. The corpse landed face down on the cabin floor. That way, those inside couldn't see the wounds in the dead man's chest and stomach. But they *could* see the large hole Malone's bullet had made coming out the back of the gunman's skull.

Malone strode in past the corpse, his grin insane. He went straight to Walter Payne, who was staring in stunned horror at the corpse on the floor and trying to shove himself backward into the wall.

Malone crouched and stuck the gun against Payne's mouth. "You got *one second* to start talking, Payne!"

Payne tore his eyes from the blasted skull of the man Malone had shot and looked into Malone's flushed, contorted face.

And suddenly Walter Payne was more frightened of this crazy cop than of Capone.

"I won't ask again!" Malone screamed at him.

"Don't!" Payne bleated. "Please—wait! I'll tell you!"

Captain Ardley turned on his heel and marched out of the cabin.

Eliot walked out after him.

The Mountie officer's expression was stony as he turned to face him. "I do *not* approve of your methods."

Eliot got out a cigarette and lit it. "Yes, well, you're not from Chicago."

TWENTY-TWO

The flat surface of a rare dead-calm Lake Michigan gleamed like a purplish mirror shot through with gold by a spectacular sunset as the Tri-Motor winged over it, bringing them back to Chicago.

Eliot spotted a familiar figure already out on the field when they landed, waiting with his camera. Ferguson, the reporter who'd snapped that embarrassing picture of him with the Japanese parasol in his hand and that silly look on his face. Eliot wasn't too surprised to see him there. That first experience had taught him that Ferguson tended to find out what was happening earlier than most.

Eliot was first out of the plane, with the handcuffed and deeply frightened Walter Payne, followed by Stone, Wallace, and Malone. Stone, conspicuous in his head bandage, shrugged away efforts to help him down from the Tri-Motor. He was still a bit unsteady from the concussion, but not enough to let himself be treated like an invalid.

Ferguson hurried to Eliot with a welcoming grin. "Congratulations on your coup at the border, Mr. Ness. Can I get a picture of you and your men?"

Eliot considered for a second. "Yes, but not for publication. Just for us. A souvenir."

"Anything you say, Mr. Ness." Ferguson got his camera ready as Eliot motioned for Malone, Wallace, and Stone to line up beside him in front of the plane.

Eliot pushed Payne a step to one side. "I don't want him in the picture," he warned Ferguson.

"If that's how you want it," Ferguson assured him, and snapped the picture.

Malone immediately stepped up to him and pulled the camera out of his hand.

"Hey!"

"Don't worry," Malone told him, "you'll get your camera back." He began removing the film from it, to make certain Ferguson didn't make copies of the picture or try taking others on the sly, especially of Walter Payne. He was slipping the film in his pocket and giving back the camera when a Ford sedan came across the field to them.

Eliot stiffened in alarm when he saw it was Malone's cousin, Sean, at the wheel—alone in the car. "What are you doing here?" he demanded when Sean brought the Ford to a stop beside him. "Are my wife and daughter . . . ?"

"They're fine, Mr. Ness. Your wife went into labor just over an hour ago, so I took her to the hospital. And I left your daughter with my wife on the way here to fetch you."

Eliot strode around the car to get in front beside Sean. "Let's go."

Malone made a quick choice between two responsibilities. Stone and Wallace, he decided, could take care of themselves—and Walter Payne—for a while without him. Eliot, on the other hand, was likely to be too preoccupied with his wife giving birth—and the newborn baby, when it arrived—to give any potential danger sufficient attention.

"Hold it a second!" he told Sean, and turned back to Stone and Wallace. "Take Payne to the U.S. district attorney and put the gears in motion for an indictment. I'll meet you there or at headquarters and we'll move Payne someplace for safekeeping until trial. If I can't get to you soon enough, I'll phone and tell you where to stash him."

He left them to it and jumped into the back seat of the Ford. It took off while he was still slamming the door shut.

In ancient times, those who brought unhappy tidings to the rulers of Rome sometimes had to bear the brunt of the Caesars' wrath. Al Capone had been called a new Caesar—for his temperament as well as his empire—by a number of journalists. The bearer of this particular piece of bad news was Jack "Machine-Gun" McGurn, who had killed some twenty rival torpedoes since joining the Capone organization. But as he came out of the cold dusk into the Lexington Hotel, his gut was knotted with a nervousness he'd never experienced in any of those gunfights.

Capone was seated at an ornate tea table in the lavish drawing room of his fourth-floor suite, gorging himself on an extravagant helping of extra-rich strawberry shortcake. He eased down a big mouthful with a sip of coffee when McGurn came in.

"What's up?" he asked McGurn contentedly.

McGurn suddenly realized he was still wearing his hat and buttoned overcoat. He took off his hat. Holding it in both hands he told Capone, haltingly, what had happened to the liquor shipment crossing the Canadian border.

Capone came to his feet with an enraged scream. *"What!"*

McGurn swallowed hard and tried to repeat the essence of the bad news. "They got the shipment . . . and Payne, too. Nobody knows where they took Payne, but I got a couple guys out trying to locate him and—"

Capone kicked over the tea table, scattering crockery, coffee, and gobs of moist pastry all over the thick Persian carpet. *"Am I alone in the world, you stupid fuck? Did I ask you what you're trying to do?"*

"No, Al, I—"

Closing the distance between them in two fast strides, Capone punched McGurn in the face with considerable force.

McGurn stumbled backward a few steps with his nose and mouth bleeding profusely. He had been a pro boxer with a string of knockouts to his record before going to work for Capone. But he made no move to strike back. Didn't even think it. He just stood there with his head bowed and the blood dripping from his face onto the front of his costly suit and the hat he was still holding in both hands.

"Go get Frank Nitti up here," Capone snapped at him, "and let's get this thing done *right*."

McGurn nodded quickly and hurried out. Not until he was in the corridor outside the suite did he take out a handkerchief and dab at his bleeding lips and nose.

Capone stalked to the corner liquor cabinet and downed two stiff shots of bourbon while he waited, working to clear his head of the boiling fury. He had it under control by the time Frank Nitti came in.

He told him what Eliot Ness had done to him at the border, in a voice that was low but charged with enough voltage to light up the whole city. Nitti listened with no change at all in his ugly, chilling face.

When Capone was finished, Nitti said, "Payne's not the strongest guy in the world. If they get time to work on him long enough he could break and spill his guts. I'll spread all our guys around the town, hunting till they find out where they got him."

"And all those people I've had on the pad for years," Capone said, "some of them're in the right spots to help with that. Make 'em *earn* that dough they get from me."

Frank Nitti nodded. "And this Eliot Ness?"

Capone's control slipped. His meaty fists clenched and his eyes bulged from the sudden buildup of pressure inside him. "I want you to get that nancy-boy where he *breathes*! I want to see his house burnt to the ground, with him and his family inside it! I want to go there in the middle of the night and piss in the ashes! I want..."

He stopped himself, taking deep breaths until he got himself calmer.

"Just tell the men," he said very softly, "whichever of them finds Eliot Ness first, I don't care how they do it, just so long as that sonofabitch winds up *dead*."

TWENTY-THREE

The lights burned late that night in the offices of U.S. District Attorney Ralph Morgan. The D.A. was a dignified, firm-voiced gentleman of sixty, unusually lean and tall. He towered over Oscar Wallace, seated beside him at Morgan's wide desk. They'd been there for hours. Wallace was taking the district attorney through every detail of the coded entries in Walter Payne's ledgers, referring regularly to his own notebook, which contained the keys Payne had given him to the codes.

The district attorney's expression remained a conflict of eager hope and wary skepticism. He'd had too much experience in pushing what seemed to be strong cases, only to have them dissolve on him in court. He needed a lot of reassurance, and Wallace was trying his best to give it to him.

"And these code words that begin with the letter A," Morgan asked yet again, "they all stand for Al Capone?"

Wallace nodded emphatically. "No matter what the rest of the letters in any group are—and those change haphazardly—if it begins with an A it equals Capone. And we have the testimony of the man who made these entries on that," he added, gesturing to the closed door to the D.A.'s private waiting room.

In that other room, Walter Payne lay on a leather-padded bench with one wrist handcuffed to its armrest. His eyes were shut, but he wasn't asleep. He was depleted by emotional fatigue, yet his brain wouldn't cease its exploration of a suddenly bleak and scary future.

A second door in the small waiting room led to the outer offices of the district attorney's staff. Like the door to Morgan's private office it was closed. The only other person in the waiting room was Stone. He sat beside Payne's bench, erect and alert despite a throbbing headache that had developed under his bandages as the night grew longer. His jacket was unbuttoned, and his hand stayed near the gun holstered to his belt. His dark eyes seldom strayed from that second door.

Its handle began being turned by someone on the other side. Stone drew his gun and was on his feet by the time the door began to open. "Who is it?"

"It's me," said the D.A.'s secretary, and pushed the door all the way open. She was carrying a tray with coffee service for two. Smiling at Stone, she went past him to the inner office. Stone's dark eyes followed her. She had great legs. Great everything.

She came out a moment later, shutting the connecting door to the D.A.'s office behind her, and smiled at Stone again. "Quite sure you won't have some, too?"

He shook his head, and his eyes followed her again, out through the second door. It was easier to concentrate on his duty after that door closed behind her.

Inside the district attorney's office, Oscar Wallace had pulled over a sheet of paper and was adding up a list of figures from Payne's income ledger, decoded with the aid of the notebook. "There you have it, sir," Wallace told Morgan, "figures totaling, in this month alone, over a quarter of a million dollars dispersed to Al Capone."

Wallace gestured again at the door to the waiting room, adding, "And we have the testimony of Walter Payne, Capone's bookkeeper, that he delivered much of the money himself."

The D.A. took the sheet of paper and studied it.

"You have a clear case, Mr. District Attorney," Wallace said emphatically. "Proof that Capone falsified his income in order to avoid paying his taxes, while earning sums like these."

The D.A. put the paper down and looked at Wallace. "You're quite certain this man Payne will testify just as you've said?"

"Yes, sir. Mr. Ness feels Payne has no alternative. For one thing, it's the only way he can avoid going to prison for a long time himself. For another, Payne burnt his bridges the moment he translated these coded entries for us. When Capone learns that his bookkeeper betrayed him—well, Payne will be safer with Capone in prison."

"And why should I indict *now*?"

"We feel you should indict now," Wallace said, "because you have both the evidence and the testimony. The ledgers would be worthless without testimony, of course. But we do have the witness ready to testify. And frankly," he added, "until Capone is behind bars—well, frankly, we can't keep Payne safe forever."

Ralph Morgan heaved a small sigh. "The maximum sentence for tax evasion would be only seven years."

"You try Capone on four counts."

The D.A. considered that point. "And this is what Mr. Ness says?"

"Yes, sir. It is."

The district attorney still couldn't shake off the nagging worry. "But if we take Capone to court for falsifying his income to avoid taxes and we *lose*, then we are going to be a laughingstock." He spent some time alone with that unpleasant prospect and concluded that he needed more assurance. "Where *is* Mr. Ness?"

"I am instructed to say," Wallace told him, "that he is on a mission of some urgency."

That urgent mission didn't let up until nine in the morning.

Eliot stood beside his wife's maternity ward bed smiling down at Catherine holding their newborn child. "Very pretty, Mrs. Ness."

"Me—or her?"

"The two of you together."

"Sure you're not sorry it's another daughter, instead of a boy this time?"

"I happen to be a man who likes girls. The more the merrier."

Catherine laughed sleepily. "Good Lord, you're going to get spoiled in a few years. *Three* girls competing for your attention."

"I'll try to face that fate with courage."

They went on smiling at each other for a time, with no words needed. Then Catherine said, "And now you've got to get back to work."

"Yes."

"Are you being careful?"

"Careful as mice," he assured her.

"And are you making progress?"

"Progress? Mrs. Ness, I think your husband just became The Man Who Got Al Capone."

Malone stood on the front hospital steps, waiting for Eliot. He had been there, and every other vulnerable point around and inside the hospital, all night. Not much different, Malone thought, than what he'd been doing most of his adult life. Standing, prowling, keeping watch. A cop's life.

On the street below him a taxicab stopped at the curb. Malone studied its driver and passenger quickly, automatically judging their threat potential. None. The passenger was a very old man. The driver got a folded wheelchair from the back, opened it, and helped him out of the back seat and into the wheelchair. He wheeled the old man up the ramp beside the front steps.

Malone opened one of the glass entrance doors for them. The old man wheeled himself through to the interior of the hospital. The cab driver went down the steps and drove off.

A girl of about fourteen, with one leg in a metal brace, came hobbling along the sidewalk. She stopped at the bottom of the ramp and looked up, taking a couple of deep breaths.

"Want some help?" Malone called.

"No thanks, mister. I'm supposed to practice doing everything myself." The crippled girl began working her way slowly up the ramp as an ambulance cruised to a stop at the curb below the steps.

A stocky man in a long, loose white doctor's coat got down from the front seat, leaving the ambulance driver inside. Another doctor climbed out of the back of the ambulance. This one was tall and thin but wore the same kind of coat. He joined the stocky doctor and they said something to the driver, who nodded and remained behind his steering wheel.

One of the hospital's entrance doors opened and Eliot stepped out close to Malone. A young mother pushing a baby carriage was coming out behind Eliot. He held the door open for her.

The two doctors started coming up the hospital steps.

Eliot smiled down at the baby as its mother pushed the carriage past him to the top of the ramp.

Malone watched the doctors climbing the steps. He didn't like their faces. He slid a hand under his jacket.

The doctors reached inside their long white coats.

Malone threw himself sideways and down, drawing his gun and shoving Eliot off his feet at the same time. Eliot fell against the young mother's legs. She was knocked to her knees with a cry of pain, but hung on to her baby's carriage with one hand.

The two "doctors" swept machine guns out from under their coats. Earsplitting gunfire shattered the morning calm as both tommyguns let go with long, sweeping bursts. Bullets lashed over the fallen group at the top of the steps and ramp. The hospital entrance doors behind them exploded into showers of splintered glass.

Eliot came up on one hip drawing his .45 and fired a split second after Malone. Both bullets hit the same gunman—the skinny one. The shots spun and dropped him, as lifeless as the stone steps across which he sprawled.

The crippled girl climbing the ramp had come to a frozen halt, close to the stocky gunman. Swiftly, he reached out with one hand and grabbed the girl. Before Eliot and Malone could shift aim and fire, he yanked her in front of him as a living shield.

At that moment the baby carriage began to roll down the ramp. The eruption of multiple gunfire had shocked the young mother into losing her hold on it. She screamed and started up to go after it. Eliot knocked her back down as he jumped to his feet and raced down the ramp after the carriage.

Malone, lying prone at the top of the steps, was trying to get an unimpeded bead on the remaining gunman. But the stocky guy had dropped to his knees with his head down, one arm locking the squirming girl against him. Malone couldn't fire without risk of hitting the girl.

Eliot sprinted down the ramp past them and caught up with the baby carriage on the pavement, stopping it just before it would have careened out into the street. The stocky gunman turned just enough to trigger a short burst at him. Eliot was flung off his feet, his gun flying out of his hand and landing in the middle of the street.

But the turn had exposed the stocky gunman's side, just long enough. Malone fired one carefully aimed shot.

The crippled girl was suddenly free, dropping to a sitting position on a step. The gunman was rolling limply down the rest of the steps below her, dying as he rolled. Malone shoved to his feet, looking down past the bottom of the steps.

The ambulance driver had disappeared.

Eliot lay motionless on the pavement, curled on his side near the baby carriage.

Malone rushed down the steps and knelt beside him, his face gone pale with anxiety. *"Eliot!"*

Behind him, the driver came crouched around the front of the ambulance and aimed the pistol in his hand at the back of Malone's head.

The two sharp little gunshots that cracked beside Malone's ear sounded like a dry stick being snapped twice. Malone twisted his head around.

The ambulance driver lay face down in the gutter.

Malone looked back to the small gun that Eliot had brought up out of nowhere and fired past his ear. Then he looked at where Eliot had gotten the gun from—an ankle holster normally concealed by Eliot's trouser leg.

Malone drew a slow breath. "I didn't know you carried a backup gun."

"You never need it till you need it badly," Eliot said in a tone Malone had used often enough on him. "Here endeth the lesson."

TWENTY-FOUR

The shot had cut a furrow across Eliot's arm just below the shoulder. It was going to hurt like hell for a week or so, and he'd have twinges a lot longer than that, but the damage wasn't deep enough to prevent him from using the arm. The wound did, however, need to be cleaned, treated, sewed up, and bandaged. And that took time.

So while Eliot was in the hospital's emergency service getting it taken care of, Malone went down the hall and made a phone call.

Walter Payne had been moved to police headquarters by then. The move was very temporary, and politically motivated. The district attorney and the chief of police belonged to the same political party. A decision had been made that they should share in the publicity of the announcement to the press.

The announcement was formally delivered in the headquarters' main ground-floor hall. An advance tip that Capone's bookkeeper was in custody, prepared to blow the props out from under his boss, crowded the hall with a mob of news photographers and reporters. While Stone and Wallace looked on with anxious impatience, the smiling D.A. and police chief got themselves photographed flanking a handcuffed and unsmiling Walter Payne.

Then the D.A. nodded to Stone and Wallace and began his prepared speech. They got Payne out of the crush and along the hall to a front elevator. Behind them the district attorney's self-assured voice was announcing:

"A subpoena for Alphonse Capone is being issued this morning by my office for the crime of evading and conspiring to evade federal income tax."

A reporter cut in fast with the big question: "What would be the maximum Capone could be sentenced to for that?"

"If convicted on all counts, Mr. Capone could get up to fifteen years in . . ."

The elevator door closed on the rest of that. Stone and Wallace rode up to the fourth floor with Payne and took him along a corridor into the headquarters holding room. Sitting Payne down, they looked at their watches simultaneously.

"Ness and Malone should be here by now," Stone said.

Wallace nodded. "Perhaps they slipped in a side door to avoid that press crush and decided to wait in the office until we got Payne free of it."

"I'll go check the office," Stone said. "You stay here and watch this guy."

Wallace nodded again. He took up a position against the wall as Stone went out, standing next to Payne with his riot gun cradled in one arm while his other hand stayed near his holstered revolver.

Payne looked up at him tiredly. "I just hope this secret place you're taking me is safe."

"It will be," Wallace said firmly.

Payne's weariness couldn't cloak his fear. "Because if *they* find out where it is, I'm telling you, they—"

"Everything is going to be fine," Wallace assured him. "Take it easy now."

Stone, getting out of the front elevator at the second floor, hurried along the corridor toward the offices of the Eliot Ness team. As he passed the head of the stairway leading to the ground-floor hall, he could hear the press conference still in progress down there. It was the police chief's unctuous voice at work now:

". . . write an end to the reign of lawlessness which has enveloped our great city for so long. So that a man can say, when he sees terror, when he sees coercion, when he sees crime, he can say without fear, 'I will speak up!' For which I must also commend the excellent assistance of Eliot Ness and his squad of . . ."

Stone's smile was sardonic as he turned into the small Ness office suite.

Sean was on the phone at the entrance desk. Glancing up, he said quickly into the phone, "Stone just walked in." Sean passed the phone to Stone. "It's Malone."

Taking the phone, Stone listened to Malone's instructions, jotted an address on a desk pad, and promised Malone he and Wallace could handle it. When he hung up, Stone tore the address from the pad, stuck it in his pocket, and hurried back up to the holding room.

"Malone just called in," he informed Wallace. "Him and Ness got held up a while longer. Wants us to get Payne to that house he fixed to keep him hid in, right away. I got the address. They'll join us there soon's they can."

Wallace tapped Payne's shoulder. "Let's go."

As Payne got to his feet, Stone added, "Malone's got a guy at the house that'll let us in. We lock ourselves in tight and stay holed up with Payne until they get there. And we *don't* answer the phone."

Wallace nodded. "Got it."

"When Ness and Malone come, they'll call first from the corner phone booth, let it ring twice, and hang up. That's the signal it's them. Anyone knocks on the door without that two-ring signal first . . ."

Wallace finished it for him, smiling. "We come out shooting."

Stone smiled back at him. "You're kinda getting to enjoy the tactical aspects of law enforcement, aren't you, Oscar?"

"It does have moments more diverting than one comes across in accounting," Wallace admitted.

"I'll go out front and get the car," Stone told him as they left the holding room with Payne. "You take him down the back elevator to the drive-in courtyard. When you get there, *stay put*. Don't even go out into the courtyard with Payne. Just wait until I bring the car around to pick you up."

"Don't worry," Wallace said as he punched the button to summon the back elevator. "I'll be there."

The elevator came up: a big cage-type. The man operating it was a fat, unarmed pensioner cop who did odd jobs around the headquarters building. He opened the door and Wallace stepped in with Payne.

"Down to the courtyard," Stone told the pensioner cop, "and no stops on the way."

"Okay." The pensioner cop shut the door and took it down. Stone hurried off to get the car.

The elevator reached bottom and stopped. "Here y'are," the pensioner cop said.

Wallace motioned Payne to the rear of the elevator and brought his riot gun in firing position. He pointed it out the elevator door as the pensioner cop opened it.

There was a short, wide corridor outside, leading straight to the courtyard in the rear of the building.

There was nobody in the corridor. Wallace motioned Payne forward as he stepped out of the elevator. They walked the short way to the other end of the corridor. Wallace stopped Payne and then took a cautious step forward, peering around the courtyard. Nobody was in sight there, either, at the moment. Wallace stepped back beside Payne and stayed there, keeping his eyes and riot gun on the courtyard, waiting for Stone to drive in there for them.

Behind them, the pensioner cop reached into a pail of rags in a corner of the elevator—and took out a long-barreled target revolver. Resting the revolver against the frame of the elevator door to steady his aim, he fired twice.

The bullets threw Oscar Wallace forward, stumbling out into the courtyard. He fought to stay on his feet, still clutching his riot gun as he turned around with excruciating slowness.

The pensioner cop waited until Wallace had turned, and then shot twice more—hitting him in the chest and face, dropping him lifeless on the courtyard paving.

Quickly, the pensioner cop stuck the revolver back down out of sight in his pail of rags. There was no way, he was satisfied, that anyone could tell whether the dead man out there had been shot first in the front or back.

Anyone except Walter Payne. And Payne, desperately trying to escape from the unknown shooter behind him, was already running away across the courtyard.

Up in his top-floor office, Deputy Chief Mike Casey stood at his window, his hands in his pockets, watching Payne run out through the courtyard's drive-in alley. When Payne disappeared from sight, Casey turned from the window and walked out of his office, taking his time.

When Stone drove the car into the courtyard, Walter

Payne was blocks away. But Payne hadn't gone far on foot. He'd been picked up by a cruising car less than half a block from the courtyard. By someone whose invitation to get in he couldn't refuse.

As the car took him off to another part of Chicago, Payne sat rigid on the back seat, gripping his knees tightly with his scrawny hands, trying to avoid looking at Frank Nitti seated beside him.

TWENTY-FIVE

The body of Oscar Wallace had been taken away by the time Eliot and Malone got there. All that was left of him in the headquarters courtyard was an outline of his sprawled figure, chalked on the paving where he had fallen and died.

While Eliot remained in the courtyard staring down at Oscar Wallace's outline, Malone went inside the building to ask a few questions. When he came out five minutes later he found Eliot standing in exactly the same position as when he'd left him.

"Seems no one saw it happen," Malone told him. "Stone and Sean are still checking around inside there, but ..." He finished it with a hopeless shrug.

"What about the elevator operator?"

Malone shrugged again. "Says he left 'em off down here, started taking the elevator up again, heard the shots. When he came back down to see what was happening it was all over: Wallace dead and Payne gone."

"*Four* shots," Eliot said in a dead-flat voice. "They

165

shot Wallace four times, front and back. More than
needed to just put him out've action so they could spring
Payne. They wanted Wallace dead."

Malone nodded. "Seems like."

"That man Capone wants *all* of us dead. Anybody
associated with me."

"Don't worry about your wife and kids," Malone said.
"I made a call in there, put more guys on them. They'll
keep 'em under tight—"

"Who are you kidding? They aren't safe until that
man is behind bars—or dead."

Eliot's tone had remained dead-flat. Malone squinted
at him, and was disturbed by something he saw in his
eyes. Something he'd never seen there before. "You
gonna be all right, Eliot?"

Eliot didn't answer.

District Attorney Morgan came out a side door into
the courtyard, looking worried and urgent. "Mr. Ness? I
need to see you in your office for a few minutes."

Eliot walked past him without responding and went
inside headquarters.

The D.A. hurried after him, calling, "I'm sorry, Mr.
Ness, but I *must* talk to you. Immediately."

Malone stayed out in the courtyard, looking around it
and trying to work out where the killer or killers might
have hidden while waiting for Wallace and Payne to
come out. A car with a police driver pulled in through
the alley. Mike Casey came out into the courtyard and
started for the car. Then he saw Malone and stopped. He
hesitated, then came over to stand beside him, glancing
down at Wallace's outline in chalk.

"Shame what happened to your guy."

Malone nodded impatiently without looking at Casey.
He was in no mood for condolences, sincere or other-
wise.

"'Course," Mike Casey said, "I didn't really get to

know this Wallace real well. But it's *always* a crime when any guy goes down in the line of duty."

Malone looked at him, beginning to be interested in a faint undertone in Casey's voice.

"I'd hate to see something like that happen to a guy I do know," Casey said. "Somebody like you, for example, Jimmy. We known each other a real long time."

"Real long," Malone agreed, studying him.

"Sometimes," Casey said, keeping his manner casual, "it's a good idea not to get involved, Jimmy. Or to get *un*involved. To take a week off, say, and get out of the city for a while. Know what I mean?"

"What *do* you mean, Mike?"

"Like I said, we go way back together. You could use a vacation. Why'n't you put in for sick leave? I'll okay it."

"Decent of you," Malone said slowly.

"Hell, we're old friends, right?" Casey grinned, slapped Malone's arm, and got into the back of his waiting car.

Malone gazed after it thoughtfully as it drove out. He remained thoughtful as he went inside and climbed a side stairway to the second floor.

District Attorney Morgan was coming out of the offices of Eliot Ness, looking even more troubled than when he'd come to the courtyard.

"He inside there?" Malone asked him.

"No. I don't think he even listened to what I was trying to tell him. Not even the courtesy of a reply. He just kept looking at Mr. Wallace's desk, and then he suddenly turned and went out."

"Where'd he go?"

"I have no idea."

Malone did have—and he didn't like it. Abruptly, he headed for the stairway.

The D.A. called after him anxiously, "When you see Mr. Ness, tell him it's *important* we . . ."

But Malone was already on his way down to the ground floor and out of the building, moving fast.

As was customary, there were several bodyguards lounging around the lobby of the Lexington Hotel when Eliot Ness came in through the revolving doors.

None of them recognized him at first. He went by them too fast, straight to the desk. "Al Capone," he snapped at the clerk.

"If you'll state your business, sir..."

Eliot reached across the desk and grabbed the clerk by his necktie, yanking him forward. *"Get him!"*

The lobby guards began converging on Eliot. They stopped suddenly, looking toward the elevator that connected only with Capone's floor. Its door was opening.

Eliot registered the expression on the desk clerk's face. He let go of his tie and turned around.

Three extra-large bodyguards were stepping out of the elevator, followed by Al Capone and Frank Nitti. They froze when they saw Eliot advancing across the lobby toward them slowly, his face like stone.

"Well, look who's come to visit," Capone jeered. "Our fucked-up fed, Eliot Ness himself."

The three bodyguards who'd emerged from the elevator first quickly tightened their group in front of him. One of the lobby guards moved to block Eliot's path, facing him menacingly. "Something you want here?"

"My friend was killed today," Eliot said softly.

The man blocking him shrugged, playing to his mob audience. "*I* don't care."

Eliot punched him in the gut, very low. The man bent forward over his pain and his face collided with the knee Eliot jerked up. He flipped over backward with his nose smashed flat and thudded to the floor.

Eliot stepped over him, eyes fastened on Capone. The struggle to clamp down on his rage had begun shredding when he'd headed for the Lexington. Those last shreds tore now. "Come on, *Big Al*, come over here! *You want to fight, fight here! Come on, Capone—what're you, afraid to come out from behind your boys?*"

Capone's face got swollen red as the blood surged to his head. He lunged forward. Nitti grabbed and stopped him, whispering quickly, "Don't let the bum trick you into a dumb play, Al! Not here. He's finished, anyway."

"Afraid to stand up for *yourself*?" Eliot snarled. "You threaten my *family*, you kill my *friend*. But you're—"

"You *wanna* do it now?" Capone screamed. "You wanna go to the mat *now*?" He broke away from Nitti and surged forward again. Two of the big bodyguards caught his arms and dragged him back, having to use all their strength to hang on to him.

Eliot's taunting laugh was vicious. "You yellow guinea sonofabitch."

Capone, struggling to break free of his bodyguards, yelled back, "And *fuck* your stinkin' family and friends!"

Eliot's brain felt like it was exploding. His hand darted under his jacket, reaching for the holstered automatic.

Suddenly Malone was behind him, locking both arms around his and pinning them to his sides, preventing him from drawing the gun. "Not that way, Eliot!" Malone hissed softly. "Easy does it, boy. *Easy...*"

For a moment Eliot fought to break Malone's bear hug. Then, abruptly, he stopped fighting him. His head began to clear. He stood still, not drawing his gun but not taking his hand away from it either.

"Atta baby," Malone whispered. "Now let's go." He dropped a hand close to his own holstered gun. "You watch my back, I'll watch yours."

They began moving together across the lobby, the eyes of Eliot and Capone never leaving each other.

Capone stopped struggling with the bodyguards holding him. "You *fuck*," he jeered as Eliot backed way. "You got *nothing*. You're nothing but talk and a badge."

His jeer mounted to a scream as Eliot and Malone reached the entrance doors and moved through them. "You came here because you got nothing! You don't got the bookkeeper, you got *nothing* in court! *Nothing!* If you were a man you would of *done* it now! *You haven't got a thing!*"

TWENTY-SIX

At Eliot's house later that day, Malone and Stone sat in the study listening to the end of his phone discussion with District Attorney Morgan—and not liking the sound of it.

"Yes, sir," Eliot said into the phone at last, "I do understand what you're saying."

He hung up and looked at Stone and Malone. "The D.A.'s going to drop the case," he told them dully. "He says he can't be unprotected, and . . ."

Pausing, he decided there was no need to say more. Dispiritedly, he got out a cigarette and lit it.

Malone growled, "What *is* it the guy says? Let me have the rest of it."

"He says he won't make a fool out of himself. He won't go into court without a witness. So tomorrow morning, he is going to announce—"

"He's just going to quit?" Malone cut in. "Give up?"

Eliot breathed out a puff of smoke, tipped his head

back, and watched it drift toward the ceiling. "He will not go into court without a witness."

"We've still got Payne's ledgers," Stone pointed out angrily. "And Oscar Wallace's notebook, explaining the codes."

"No good by themselves, Giuseppe. Not without Payne there to testify *he* did those ledgers, and personally collected and delivered some of the monies listed in them." Eliot gave Stone a smile that was more like a grimace. "I'm afraid there comes a time when you have to cut your *losses,* when you're—"

The telephone on his desk rang. He picked it up. "Hello? Oh, hello, Catherine, how d'you feel?" Eliot paused, listening to her, and his eyes narrowed as though concealing pain. "Yes . . . No, he didn't have a family." That was a subject he didn't care to stay with. He cut it off by asking his wife, "Listen, is Cora there yet? What's she think of her new sister? Well, you give her my love. Uh-huh. I will."

Hanging up, Eliot told Malone and Stone, "Well, I think that's enough for us for today. I'll meet both of you tomorrow morning."

Stone rose uncertainly to his feet, the frustration gnawing at him. "There must be *some* way we can use those ledgers to—"

"Thank you," Eliot told him firmly. "We'll meet *tomorrow.*"

"Yes, sir." Stone gritted his teeth and left.

Malone stayed put, eyeing Eliot. "You're saying that's *it*?"

"I'm sorry."

"You heard me. My question is—*are we done?*"

"Yes, I think we're done."

"You're saying that we sat down in a game that was above our heads?"

"It does appear so," Eliot told him soberly. "It would certainly appear so to Mr. Wallace."

"Yeah, well, he's *dead*." Malone was silent for several seconds. "And the D.A.'s going to drop the case."

"He won't go into court without a live witness. He won't go into court without the bookkeeper. It's not difficult to see his point, you've got to admit."

Malone leaned back, raised his hands a bit and looked at them, then dropped them on the arms of his chair. "What did your wife want?" he asked, as though dropping the subject that had become too painful for both of them.

"She wanted to know if I was all right."

Malone's smile was nostalgic. "It's nice to be married, eh?"

"She's sitting there in bed with Cora and our new baby, and she's looking over paint charts for our kitchen back home in Washington." Eliot shook his head in wonder. "Some part of the world still cares what color the kitchen is. I understand, but at the moment it's hard to believe."

He stabbed his cigarette into the ashtray and ground it out. Malone watched him with narrowed, patient eyes, as though waiting something out.

Eliot sighed and got slowly to his feet. "Well, sir. We have fought—and we have lost."

"Not yet," Malone said quietly, as though communing with himself. "Maybe I've got one last card. Let me try playin' it. You get the D.A. back on the phone and make an appointment with him. Go talk to him in person, face to face. Get him to hold off on that announcement just a little while longer. *Stall* him."

"Stall him," Eliot repeated heavily. "Stall him with *what*?"

Malone stood up. "Just do it, Eliot. I think I can find this guy."

"Which guy are you talking about?"

"Walter Payne."

Eliot just looked at Malone for several seconds.

"Payne is almost certainly dead. He betrayed Capone when he translated those books for us, and Capone knows it. Being the kind of man he is—if you can call something like Capone a man—he must have killed Payne by now."

"Maybe, maybe not. I think not—not that fast. With all the businesses Capone's involved in, there's got to be a *lot* more account books somewhere to keep track of 'em. In code. And Payne's the bookkeeper—the one who knows what they're all about. If Payne's already dead, all those businesses'll be in a hell of a mess. Capone's *got* to keep Payne around awhile—at least till he can bring it all up to date and break some new book-keeper in on everything."

Eliot shook his head dubiously. "You're *reaching*, Malone."

"Sure. But if you don't reach, you don't *get*." Malone poked Eliot's chest with his finger. "Buy me time to find out. *Stall* the D.A."

There were several reporters and two news photographers waiting outside the Lexington Hotel for Al Capone to show up late that afternoon. There had been many more of them some hours ago. They'd all showed up at the Lexington after the same thing: any comment Capone cared to make about how the case against him would be affected by the disappearance of the government's witness, Walter Payne.

But they'd arrived to learn Capone wasn't in the hotel. Nobody there would say where he'd gone or when he'd be back. Gradually, most of the press crowd had evaporated.

Those who'd persisted, however, finally had their reward. A black limousine hove into view, approaching the Lexington.

Al Capone wouldn't be in that one, of course. When

Capone went anywhere by car, it was always in convoy, with one carload of gunmen in the lead and another bringing up the rear. Capone's car was in the middle, a quarter of a block behind the first limousine. It was instantly recognizable: a McFarland sedan converted into a traveling fortress, doubled in weight by all the armor added to protect it against attack.

The newsmen crowded close to the hotel's entrance as the lead limousine glided to the curb. Three Capone torpedoes got out. They were followed by Frank Nitty, who waved the newsmen away and told the torpedoes, "Push 'em back."

As the newsmen were shoved away from the entrance, one of them called out to Nitti, "Frank, can we just ask Capone what—"

Nitti cut him short. "You boys know the rules. Nobody bothers Mr. Capone going in. After he's all settled in upstairs, *then* you come in the lobby and ask if he feels like talking to you."

The big armored sedan pulled to a stop behind the first car. Three bodyguards jumped out and joined the torpedoes in keeping the path to the hotel entrance unobstructed. Then Al Capone climbed out.

"Al! Al!" called some newsmen, trying to slip between the gunmen to him.

"I said keep *back*," Nitti growled, and motioned the torpedoes and bodyguards to make sure they did.

Capone was crossing the pavement when one reporter called out, "Al, what about this court case against you?"

Al Capone, about to go inside, stopped and looked back. After a beat he said, "Let 'em through."

Nitti hurried to him, worried. "But Al . . ."

"I *said* let 'em through."

Nitti knew better than to argue with Capone. He nodded at the guards.

"About that question," Capone said incisively as the

newsmen were allowed through to him, "they ain't *got* no case. Just some people tryin' to mess me up."

The two photographers moved into position to take pictures of him. Always aware of cameras, Capone had the unscarred side of his face turned to them by the time the flashbulbs popped. Then he went on speaking.

"I'll tell you boys something. Somebody messes with me, I'm going to mess with *him*. Someone steals from me, I'm going to say 'you stole,' not talk to him for spitting on the sidewalk instead. You understand? Now, I have done nothing to hurt these people, but they're angered at me, so what do they do? They doctor up some creepy play, some *income tax*, for which they have no case. Just to annoy me. To speak to me like *men?* No. To *harass* a peaceful man."

The injustice of it obviously infuriated him, but Capone kept his voice calm, speaking more in sorrow than in anger. "Well, I'll tell you. I pray to God that if *I* had a grievance, I would have more self-respect."

"Al," a reporter asked, "do you think Eliot Ness will continue his crusade against you, in spite of—"

"Let him try!" Capone snapped, his anger showing itself now. "Because I'll tell you one more thing. When you got an all-out prizefight, you wait until the fight is over. *One* guy is left standing. And that's how you know who won."

With a wave of his hand and a big smile, Al Capone turned and went into the hotel, followed by Frank Nitti, torpedoes, and bodyguards. Speech delivered, interview over.

The newsmen had all gone before Frank Nitti came out again an hour later. Even if any of them had still been hanging around out in front of the Lexington, they wouldn't have seen him go.

Nitti slipped out of the Lexington via a rear door through a service alley, unseen.

He had another job to take care of for Capone. The kind of assignment he'd so often proved he knew how to handle.

TWENTY-SEVEN

Dusk had finished closing in on Chicago when Malone entered the speakeasy two blocks from headquarters. It had been a basic Irish bar before Prohibition, and it still was that. Old dark wood, sawdust on the floor, reasonably priced drinks, the customers mostly cops in uniform, of all ranks but with class distinctions ignored while they were in there.

Most of the cops knew Malone. Some looked surprised to see him out of uniform, a number greeted him with friendly grins, others got tight suspicious expressions at the sight of him. Malone strolled down the length of the bar, exchanging nods and smiles, returning hard stare for hard stare.

Beyond the end of the bar was a short corridor. It led past the toilets to a closed door with a sign on it: MEMBERS ONLY. Malone turned the knob and stepped through. The back room was cloudy with cigar and cigarette smoke, noisy with good-natured conversation. Everyone in this room was in uniform. There were cops drinking and playing cards at four tables, others standing around the pool table watching a game between Lieutenant Alderson and Deputy Chief Mike Casey.

Those who saw Malone come in fell silent. Some eyed him with sour distrust; others looked away, embarrassed.

At the pool table Mike Casey, his bent back to Malone, called his shot. "Cross-the-side, one time." He sank the shot, moved around the table, and called his next. "Two ball, down." The cue ball made a sharp click against the two ball, sending it down the table. It missed the pocket by a fraction of an inch, thudding off the cushion and rolling back.

Casey made a rueful face and straightened, stepping back as Lieutenant Alderson moved in for his turn, calling his first shot. "Nine ball, straight in."

The ball went in as Malone reached Casey's side and touched his arm. "Hello, Mike," he said softly, "you got a minute?"

Casey stiffened a bit and looked at Malone, not replying at first, very aware of all the other cops watching the two of them together.

"Got a minute?" Malone repeated. "I need to talk to you."

Alderson had sunk his second shot and was calling his third. Casey made his expression stiff, ungiving. "I'm in the middle've a game, like you see."

"Let somebody else take over for you," Malone said. "It's important to me, Mike."

"This is a club for *cops*," Casey told him, half jocularly, playing to the others in the room. "What's a fed in civvies doing in a club for *cops*?"

"I said it's important."

"So talk."

Malone nodded at a door to the back alley. "Let's step outside."

"I got nothing to say to *you*," Casey told him loudly, his expression blank.

Malone went to the door, opened it, and looked back at Casey. "Come on, Mike—for *old times' sake*."

Casey glanced around at the other cops, shrugged, gave his pool stick to one of them, and walked over to Malone. They stepped outside, Malone shutting the door behind them.

The only light in the alley came from a small bulb above the door. It was a dim, sinister light, merging into shadows a short way in either direction.

"Okay," Casey said quietly, dropping the unfriendly tone he'd put on inside, "whaddaya want, Jimmy?"

"I need a piece of information, Mike. Just one piece, to get the show back on the road for Ness."

Casey stared at him. "A piece of . . . Are you crazy? I already risked my *life* for you when I warned you to get out've town for a while. And that's advice you shoulda taken."

Malone showed no response to that. "I need to find that bookkeeper. Payne."

Casey shook his head, incredulous. "You *are* crazy. Coming to me for something like that. I done you the last favor I'm ever going to, Jimmy. If *they* knew I tried to warn you away, I'm *dead*. So forget that old-times'-sake crap. You owe *me*." He started around Malone toward the alley door.

Malone's hand closed around Casey's arm and stopped him. "I need to find that bookkeeper," he repeated mulishly.

"I wouldn't tell you even if I knew where he is. Which I don't."

"You know which people would know. Just tell me who they are, where to find them."

Mad and scared, Casey tried to wrench his arm free of Malone's grasp. Malone tightened his grip and held him there. "I got to know, Mike. One of my people got himself murdered for it."

"Your people!" Casey exploded. "*We're* your people, Jimmy."

"You're my people? You run with dagos, and then you're my people? *Mike*, they *ruined* this town! Those dagos—and you're one of 'em."

Casey forced a laugh. "Me, a dago? I'm more Irish than you are. If *I'm* Italian, you're—"

"I'm not talking about *Italians*, Mike. I'm talking about *slime*—the kind you're in with up to your eyeballs." Malone's free hand went into a pocket and came out with a badge. "You see this? This was my father's badge, this is *my* badge. For the last ten *years*, Mike, I can't eat my food, the *shit* that's going on. And I say I'm a cop..."

"Hey, bullshit—*live* in this charade, with your soft clothes and your federal stooge. Ness—what's he gonna do, clean up this town? Don't make me laugh."

"You keep your mouth off him." Malone's voice had gotten lower, with an ugly undercurrent. "With the shit you've done in your time...Okay, here's my appeal to you. I need a guy. I need to know where this guy is. Now you help me find him—or *for old times' sake* I'm gonna rat you out. I mean it. For all the shit I know you've done in your life. I'm going to turn you over—give the works on you to the governor, the feds, the newspapers."

Casey's eyes narrowed to slits, peering through the alley's gloom at Malone for several seconds. Then he said softly, "We've been *friends*, Jimmy."

"*Been*—that's past tense, ain't it? Long past."

"You'd really do that. To me."

"*Believe* it."

"You dirty fink bastard..." Casey kicked Malone's shin, broke loose, and clouted Malone's jaw, dropping him into the grimy trash of the alley.

Malone rubbed his jaw and looked up at Casey with a crooked grin. He came back on his feet fast, feinting a left at Casey's eyes and sinking a right into his stomach. Casey gasped and sagged against the alley wall, then shoved away from it swinging. Malone took two punches to get in close, slugged Casey in the kidney and then his heart, brutal blows that battered him to the ground.

Standing over him, Malone said thinly, "Let's cut the woofing, pal. You tell me what you know or you're going to the hospital before you go to jail. You think I'm bluffing, you stand up again."

Casey kicked Malone's ankles out from under him. Malone toppled over him. The two of them rolled in the alley using knees, fists, elbows on each other. When they broke and surged to their feet they were both panting. But Casey's panting was harsher than Malone's.

Malone regarded him malevolently. "You used to be tougher, Mike. But you've done too many years on your butt behind a desk, while I been outside walking."

He waded in, deflecting Casey's punch, and clubbed him twice across the ear with the side of his fist, very hard. Casey went down on his hands and knees, groaning, head sagging. Then, slowly and painfully, he began shoving himself back up.

Malone waited until Casey was all the way up before knocking him down again.

Two hours later, on the other side of the city, Malone used a corner phone booth to make several calls. His clothes were still torn and filthy from the battle with Casey, his lips and one eye swollen. The last number he tried was the home of Stone's parents. Stone's mother answered, and called her son to the phone.

"Do you know where Ness is?" Malone asked him.

"No, I—"

"I called his house, but he's not there. Sean's guarding the place but doesn't know where he went. I tried the office and his wife's hospital room, but . . . Listen, Giuseppe, go to the office and leave a message for him to call his house if he shows up there. Then get over to his house. Sean'll let you in. Stay put until Ness joins you. Then *both* of you stay put till I call."

"What's happening?"

"I got a lead," Malone told him. "I'm following it up. Could take all night. I want you both where I can get you fast if it pans out."

For Eliot, tracking down U.S. District Attorney Morgan had been more time-consuming than he had anticipated. The D.A. had gone home from his office, but Eliot got to the D.A.'s house only to learn he'd left there, too. The district attorney had a number of social functions to attend that evening. No one seemed to know in what order he'd be attending them, so Eliot had to visit most of them before learning that the D.A. had gone off to a late supper with a few friends. Nobody was able to tell Eliot where.

It was midnight when the district attorney returned home. He found Eliot outside, waiting for him. The D.A. was sleepy and eager to get to bed. But he was also a well-bred gentleman, and basic politeness forced him to invite Eliot inside.

Sitting in the D.A.'s downstairs library, Eliot finally got to say his piece. "That announcement you've scheduled for first thing in the morning, sir. I'm here to ask you—to beg you—to put if off. If you drop the case now it will be extremely difficult to turn around and bring the same charges against Capone at a later time."

"That's true, of course," the D.A. acknowledged. "But—"

"I'm just asking you to hold off for a *little* longer. To hang on and give us a chance. I've reason to believe the case may not be as lost as it seems to you at this moment. Give us a bit more time and we may be able to give *you* reason to fight this thing out."

"Yes, I can understand that you *want* to believe that," the district attorney said, in a kindly tone. "And I would certainly *like* to be able to fight it out, as you put it. But, again, on what basis?"

The D.A. stifled a yawn, excused himself, and looked at Eliot regretfully. "You must understand, Mr. Ness, I have a certain standing to protect. If I don't drop those charges promptly—first thing in the morning, as I plan to—and find myself having to admit later that I have, in fact, no case—well, I can't risk making a fool of myself like that."

"Don't tell me, sir," Eliot rasped, "don't tell me about making a fool of yourself."

District Attorney Morgan stiffened in his chair, and Eliot quickly stopped himself. His temper seemed to be getting the better of him too often lately. Add that to the long list of Al Capone's evil influences. Eliot brought his voice down:

"I'm sorry, sir. But *you* must understand. I have men out there who are risking something more than that. I'm told that we have an important *lead*, and we're following that lead at this moment. Under conditions that endanger more than our *standing*. But we need your continued support. *Don't* quit now."

TWENTY-EIGHT

It was still dark out when Malone let himself into his house at 1634 Racine, but dawn was not far off.

His puffed eye and torn mouth were not the only mementos of the fight with Mike Casey. The body bruises were now aching badly enough to slow his movements, and he was dead tired—reminders that he'd been a young man the last time he'd had a knock-down drag-out alley brawl.

He needed a stiff drink to pick him up. He also needed a quick hot bath and a change of clothes. But first he needed to make a call. Picking up the phone in his living room, Malone dialed Eliot Ness's home number.

There was a faint extra click on the line when Eliot picked up at his end and said, "Hello?"

Malone said quickly, "Watch what you say. Somebody may have a tap on your phone."

"Sounds possible," Eliot said carefully. "Did you find it?"

"It" being Walter Payne.

"I don't know where it *is*," Malone answered with equal care, "but I think I know where it's gonna be later."

"Where are you?"

"My place. You and Stone meet me here. We got a little time. Not much, but it should be enough."

"We'll be there."

Malone hung up and trudged into his kitchen, got the whiskey bottle from the cupboard, and poured a large glass half full. Setting the bottle on the sideboard near the sink, he took a big swallow from the glass, wincing as the alcohol attacked cuts in his gums.

He carried the glass into the bathroom, put it on the ledge beneath the mirror, stuck the plug in the tub, and turned on the hot-water faucet all the way. As steam began to rise from the tub, Malone opened the other faucet a little, adding just enough cold water to the stream so the bath wouldn't scald the skin off him. Then he trudged to his bedroom.

Back when his wife was alive, their bedroom had been upstairs, at the back of the second floor. When she died, Malone hadn't had the heart to go on sleeping in that same room he'd shared with her. So he'd put a bed in what had been her sewing room, near the rear of the ground floor. Just until he got over the loss, he'd thought. But as it had turned out, he still slept down here.

Malone took off his cap and jacket and dumped them on the easy chair, got fresh clothes from the closet and drawers, and laid them on the bed. He stripped off his belt, dropping it with his holstered revolver on the bed. Kicking off his shoes, he added his trousers to the chair. The tiredness was getting so pervasive his brain was threatening to close up business entirely. He trudged back into the steaming bathroom, picked up the glass, and finished off the rest of the whiskey in it.

That helped a bit. He glanced at the tub. Still only a quarter full. Trouble with old houses: low water pressure. Malone carried the empty glass through the living room and into the kitchen, poured more whiskey in it, and had another drink. Better and better. Carrying both the glass and bottle, he headed back toward the bathroom.

As he reentered the living room, Malone found himself confronting an intruder, a small dark man holding a long shiny stiletto.

The man stood in the center of the room. He looked puny, but he faced Malone with a very sure smile, and his stance was that of an experienced knife fighter: slightly crouched, feet apart just enough for good balance and quick shifts, the stiletto held forward at gut level, its wickedly sharp point moving in tiny circles.

Malone threw the glass at him, making him jump back and sideways to avoid getting the spray of whiskey in his eyes. That gave Malone the moment he needed. He gripped the neck of the bottle and smashed its bottom across the corner of a side table. What he had in his hand then was a fairly formidable weapon, bristling with shards of jagged glass.

The knife fighter circled closer warily: not afraid of that weapon, but cautious. A broken bottle wasn't in the same killing class as a stiletto; but it could do serious damage, especially if slashed across a man's face or hands.

Malone circled in the other direction, always facing his opponent with the jagged bottle held up to ward him off. The knife fighter suddenly sidestepped and lunged forward, feinting at Malone's face to bring the bottle up and then jabbing the stiletto at Malone's stomach. But Malone didn't fall for the feint. He dodged just enough to avoid the knife thrust and slashed the jagged bottle at the other's eyes.

The knife fighter reversed direction swiftly, leaping

backward one step. Malone jerked his weapon back into position quickly, deterring another stiletto lunge.

Then they were circling each other again, the circles getting tighter. When Malone reached a certain point in the middle of the living room he stopped circling and began backing up.

The knife fighter came after him, closing the distance between them by wary inches, the long-bladed stiletto ready for the kill. Malone stopped again when he felt the gramophone against his back. He reached behind him with his left hand, flipped open the gramophone's lid, and reached inside.

The little man with the stiletto had come to a halt, not understanding and not liking what he didn't understand.

Malone's hand brought out the sawed-off shotgun, his finger sliding across the trigger as he aimed it.

"Now ain't that just like a dago," Malone said pleasantly, "bringing a knife to a gunfight."

The knife fighter began to back off quickly, through the archway into the entry. Malone tossed his broken bottle aside and walked steadily after him with the aimed shotgun. The knife fighter was halted by his back coming against the wall on the other side of the entry.

"Drop the knife," Malone ordered, "and get your hands up over your head, empty and real high."

The knife fighter licked his dry lips and forced his hand to open. The stiletto fell on the entry rug.

"Nice boy," Malone said, and stepped through the archway into the entry.

Frank Nitti was waiting seven feet to his right, sitting on the stairs holding a .38 pistol with a silencer in both hands, his elbows braced on his raised knees to keep his aim steady.

"Hello, Malone," Frank Nitti said. "Good-bye, Malone."

Malone twisted around toward him with the shotgun.

But he was slowed by weariness and the painful bruises and just plain age.

Or maybe he had never been fast enough for what he was trying to do in that brief moment.

Not against someone like Frank Nitti, who already had the drop on him before Malone even began his turn.

TWENTY-NINE

The front door of Malone's house had been left slightly open. Eliot was reminded sharply of the night he'd rushed to his informer's apartment and found the door the same way. He had the same sinking feeling as he pushed the door all the way open and stepped inside with his gun drawn, followed by Stone.

Malone was stretched out on his back in the entry, in his shirt, underpants, and socks. He was staring at the ceiling with wide-open eyes that didn't see it or anything else.

There was a bullet entrance wound in his right temple, and another in his forehead, just above the bridge of his nose.

That wasn't all. A knife had slashed Malone's throat from ear to ear.

Stone froze beside Eliot, staring unbelievingly at Malone. "Holy Mother of God," he whispered in Italian. "What have they done to you, my friend?"

As though his legs had abruptly drained of strength,

he sat down on the entry floor beside the dead man. He reached and touched Malone's bloody face with his fingertips, while tears streamed down his own.

Eliot moved on through the house, leading the way with his gun, checking on whether the killers were still there. He was fairly sure they wouldn't be, and they weren't. After searching the ground floor he did the top floor. They were gone. When he came back down the stairs, Stone was still sitting on the floor by Malone's body, weeping.

"You can cry over him later," Eliot told him thickly. "There's the job to do first. He said he learned where Payne will be. Maybe he marked it down somewhere. Help me look."

Stone didn't respond, didn't raise his bowed head.

"You want what Malone did for us to be a waste?" Eliot demanded harshly. "You want him to have died for *nothing*?"

He left the entry and crossed the living room to the bathroom. Turning off the water still running in the tub, he straightened and looked around him. There was nothing that caught his attention. When he stepped back into the living room Stone was standing there, waiting for him.

"The bedroom in back first," Eliot said. "The clothes he was wearing are there."

They went into the ground-floor bedroom. Taking Malone's discarded trousers from the easy chair, Eliot began going through its pockets. Stone picked up the crumpled jacket from the same chair and started emptying its pockets on the bed. He paused in the middle of doing so, looking at the holstered gun Malone had dumped on the bed.

After a moment, Stone drew the gun out of its holster, automatically checked that it was fully loaded, and stuck it in his belt under his jacket. A gun was a weird keepsake to remember a friend by. But in Malone's case, maybe not. Without allowing himself to dwell on that longer, Stone continued to go through the jacket.

Eliot found no note of any kind in Malone's trouser pockets. Only the usual: door and car keys, a small amount of paper money and some loose change, a rosary, Malone's callbox key chain with its Saint Jude medallion. Eliot put that last in his own pocket.

Behind him, Stone wondered aloud, "Why'd he have *this*?"

Eliot turned and saw he was holding a train schedule. Taking it from Stone's hand, he opened it.

One of the printed entries was circled in pencil.

It was for an early-morning passenger train out of Northwestern Station.

The entry read: "Departs 6:04 A.M."

Eliot looked at his watch. The time was close, but they could make it if they headed for the station immediately.

Seconds later he and Stone were back in their car, racing away from the house where Malone had lived and died.

At ten minutes before six that morning, two well-dressed, strongly built men with hard faces were among the passengers boarding a first-class carriage of the train scheduled to depart from the Northwestern Station in fourteen minutes. Each had booked an entire compartment to himself. Their compartments were on either side of a third that was still unoccupied.

Each of these two men carried only a single bag. Leaving those in their separate compartments, they climbed back down from the train and stood a little apart, studying every other person in sight along the platform. They saw nothing to worry about. They seemed to give no special attention to a small group that approached along the platform at 5:56 A.M.

The group consisted of a nun pushing an invalid in a

wheelchair, accompanied by a priest and two porters carrying four suitcases. The invalid was a small man wrapped in a large blanket that covered even his lower face. He wore a hat tilted low over his forehead, shadowing his eyes.

When they reached the carriage where the two hard-faced men stood, the priest showed the porters the compartment number on his reservation forms. While the porters carried the suitcases aboard, the nun bent to wish the invalid a good trip. Then she nodded good-bye to the priest and hurried away.

The two porters came out of the carriage to take the invalid aboard. As they lifted him out of his wheelchair, one of the hard-faced men on the platform turned and climbed back aboard. The other continued to stand watch as the invalid was carried into the carriage.

The priest remained beside the empty wheelchair, glancing up and down the platform. The other passengers hurrying past the priest were too sleepy that early in the morning to give him more than a casual glance. Even had they been more wide-awake, it was unlikely any of them would have noticed the bulge of the submachine gun slung under his cassock.

Having deposited the invalid in the compartment he was sharing with the priest, the porters came out to carry the wheelchair aboard. The priest accompanied them to the compartment, tipped them liberally, and settled into the seat across from the invalid.

At 6:02 A.M. the train conductor strode along the platform warning the few passengers still outside to say their last good-byes and get aboard. The hard-faced man who'd remained on the platform waited until the last of the other passengers were inside and the people who'd come to see them off were walking away. Then he climed into the carriage and went along the corridor.

His partner was stationed outside the closed door of

the compartment containing the invalid and priest. "It's okay," he told him. "All clear. No problem."

Outside, at the end of the train, the brakeman looked up from his watch and signaled. At exactly 6:04 A.M. the train began pulling out of the station.

Inside the compartment, Walter Payne unwrapped the blanket that had covered him, took off his hat, got his thick glasses from his pocket and put them on.

Across from him, the torpedo dressed as a priest continued to look out the compartment window, checking to make sure nobody came rushing across the platform to jump aboard the slow-moving train at the last second.

Nobody did.

The train picked up speed as it left the station behind.

At that moment Eliot and Stone sat fuming in their motionless car at the wrong end of the 22nd Street Bridge. It had been 5:58 when they'd reached that point, with just enough time left to make it the rest of the way to the station before the train left. But they had to cross the bridge to do that, and they couldn't. The bridge had been going up to let a high-stacked tugboat pass through along the Chicago River underneath, blocking traffic in both directions.

Eliot gripped the steering wheel as he watched the two halves of the bridge finally descending, with the smoke from the tugboat's stack drifting back between them. Beside him, Stone consulted his watch. It was 6:06.

"It's too late," he said grimly. "We already missed it. Pulled out two minutes ago."

"What's the next station on that line?" Eliot asked him tensely.

Stone consulted the train schedule. He read off the name of a small suburban station, just outside the city. "But this train doesn't make a stop there."

"We'll see about that." Eliot accelerated across the bridge the instant its two halves met, took a sharp turn on the other side of it, and sped in and out of the early-morning traffic to get out of the city to that suburban station on time.

THIRTY

Aboard the train, Walter Payne gazed emptily at the outskirts of Chicago flashing past his compartment window and tried to quell another jolt of the terror that kept driving him to helpless panic.

Across from him the alert-eyed gunman in the priest costume slid the submachine gun from under his cassock. It was fitted with a twenty-round box magazine. He put it on the seat beside him and covered it with the blanket he'd taken from Payne. His name was Rudensky, and he'd been put in charge of the three-man bodyguard team assigned to get Payne from Chicago to Miami. It was a sound choice. Rudensky's experience in protecting underworld figures was almost as impressive as his proficiency in disposing of them.

"I was told you got a lot of bookkeeping to get finished before we get to Florida," he said to Payne. "Wanna get started on it?"

Payne tried to reply, but the words got caught in his throat. He made do with a nod.

Rudensky was opening a suitcase to get out the book-keeper's briefcase when knuckles rapped a signal on the door: one knock, pause, then two knocks. Rudensky unlocked the door. The other two bodyguards came in to join them, one carrying his bag. Wearing hats, they'd looked enough alike to be brothers. Without the hats one was blond and the other dark-haired, but they still looked alike.

Rudensky relocked the door and handed Payne the briefcase. Unlocking it, Payne took out a ledger and a notebook. Getting a pen from his breast pocket, he began consulting the ledger and jotting notes in the other book. It was at least something to occupy his mind, to distract himself from the fear.

The trouble was, this work Capone wanted him to do was one more source of that fear.

There would be another, younger bookkeeper waiting to meet him in Florida. Payne was supposed to explain all the accounts and coding systems to him.

Capone had explained that Payne was getting too old to go on working so hard all the time. Payne needed an assistant bookkeeper who understood those business records as well as Payne, Capone had said, so Payne could take a vacation now and then.

The explanation didn't help Payne shake the suspicion that the new bookkeeper had been hired to take over the accounts permanently, and that his vacation was also intended to be permanent, and fatal.

Payne had tried his best to explain to Capone his momentary failure of nerve under pressure from Malone and Ness. And Capone had replied that he understood—and forgave. But the fact was, Payne hadn't even been able to get to *see* Capone ever since he'd been snatched away from headquarters. Everything Payne wanted to tell Capone, and everything Capone had to say in return, was passed through Frank Nitti.

Payne was sure of the reason for that: Capone was so

mad he knew he couldn't conceal it if they met face to face.

"It's just that Al is too busy right now with some other stuff," Nitti had reassured him. "Don't worry about it."

But Walter Payne did worry about it. And he continued to do so, in spite of concentrating determinedly on his bookkeeping, as the train carried him out of Chicago.

Stone braced his feet against the floor of the car as Eliot executed a screeching turn over a short bridge into a small residential community outside Chicago. They went up a hill with the gas pedal jammed down as far as it could go. When they topped the hill they saw the train approaching in the distance. The car sped down the hill toward the station.

The red warning lights began flashing at the railroad crossing as they approached it. Eliot slowed but did not stop—not until they went past the warning lights. Then he practically stood on the brakes. The car came to a bucking halt, stalling square in the middle of the tracks.

Eliot was out of it before the shaken Stone, sprinting toward the little station building.

There were several people inside transacting business at the ticket window when he burst in. Flashing his badge and drawing his automatic with his other hand, he yelled at them, "Everybody out! Get the hell out of here! *Away* from the track! *Now!*"

Whether it was the badge, the gun, or the wildness of his voice that was most potent, there was a panicked exodus to the street side of the station. Eliot ran out the track-side door and almost collided with Stone.

The approaching train began to blast its whistle repeatedly. The engineer had seen the car on the tracks ahead. The train began to slow as he slammed on the brakes.

"Jump the first passenger car and work back," Eliot instructed Stone. "I'll work forward from the last car."

He was off as he finished saying it, running alongside the tracks. Stone drew the gun from his holster as he headed in the opposite direction.

Inside Payne's compartment, the sudden slowing of the train had them all wondering. "What the hell," the blond bodyguard muttered. "We ain't supposed to stop here."

"Maybe got a signal to pick somebody up at this station," the dark-haired one said.

"Yeah, but *who*?" Rudensky gestured to Payne. "Get that stuff back in your briefcase and be set to move out fast if we have to." He pulled down the compartment's window shade. If it *was* trouble waiting for them out there, he didn't want the source of that trouble spotting their exact location on the train.

The blond bodyguard was already opening his bag, reaching inside for a short-barreled shotgun. Rudensky passed the tommy gun to the other bodyguard and put off drawing the revolver holstered under his priest's cassock. He might need both hands free to drag Payne out of there quickly enough.

The train squealed to a halt less than fifteen feet from the car straddling the tracks. In the same instant Stone jumped onto the first of the passenger cars and Eliot swung up onto the end of the last one.

The last one turned out to be an observation car. Eliot moved forward between the rows of seated passengers, flashing his badge and warning them to stay where they were. His finger tensed across the trigger of his gun as he reached the end of the observation car. Opening the door at its front end, he stepped out onto the between-cars platform and looked through the window of the next car's rear door.

It was a dining car. He opened the door and went through it swiftly, barely glancing at the passengers at the tables. If Payne was aboard this train, his keepers wouldn't have him out in plain sight.

A waiter was at the front end of the car, preparing an order. Eliot asked him, "What's the next car?"

"First-class compartments," the waiter told him. "What's going on?"

"Get back and sit down," Eliot warned him sharply as he moved past and opened the door. Stepping out, he peered through the rear-door window of the next car.

Its corridor was empty. All the compartment doors were closed. Eliot opened the car's rear door and started to advance through it.

Halfway down the corridor, a compartment door opened slightly. Not enough for Eliot to see inside the compartment. What he did see was the shotgun barrel that came poking out of that opening.

Eliot didn't even try to get in a first shot with his own gun. Payne could be inside that compartment, and he needed him alive. What he did do was to hurl himself down backward, slamming the door shut as he dropped. The shotgun boomed as he fell on the platform between the cars. The spreading load of shot smashed through both car-door windows above him. It scattered through the dining car, hitting the waiter who hadn't obeyed fast enough and a passenger rising to see what was happening.

In the compartment car the shotgunner stepped out into the corridor, keeping his weapon trained on the rear door behind which Eliot lay hidden. The bodyguard with the submachine gun came out of the compartment next, followed by Rudensky carrying the briefcase in one hand and dragging Payne along with his other.

Rudensky nodded toward the front end of the car. "Out that way. We'll grab a car."

The machine gunner led the way up the corridor, moving fast. Rudensky hustled Payne along after him. The shotgunner backed slowly after them, keeping his eyes and weapon on that rear door. The machine gunner opened the front door and jumped out onto the station platform, ready to mow down any visible threat. Spotting none, he signaled the all-clear. Rudensky climbed down with Payne.

Eliot, keeping himself flat between the cars, reached up his left hand and opened the compartment car's rear door a few cautious inches. The shotgunner, backing to the front door, spotted it and lowered his weapon to send a blast through the opening before Eliot could see him. But he didn't get to squeeze the shotgun's trigger.

Stone, working his way back through the train, stepped into the front end of the next passenger car in that instant. He whipped up his gun and fired, very fast. One shot. The Police Academy rangemaster had been right about his prowess. The bullet went through two car-door windows and into the back of the shotgunner's head.

Out on the station platform, the bodyguard with the tommy gun swung around and triggered a long burst that swept across Stone's position in the train, shattering a succession of windows there and forcing Stone to fling himself to the floor.

The burst ended abruptly when Eliot swung himself partway out from between the two train cars and snapped off three shots at the machine gunner. The first missed. The second slashed his hip and twisted him off his feet. The third broke his spine as he fell.

Rudensky dashed inside the station, yanking the fear-paralyzed bookkeeper with him.

Stone leaped from the train and ran in after them, with Eliot a few steps behind him. They came to a halt, side by side, just inside the door. Rudensky had dropped the briefcase to the floor and was standing behind Payne with one arm locked around his neck. His other hand held a revolver to Payne's head.

"I'm going out with the bookkeeper," Rudensky told them flatly, "and we're gonna drive away. You two drop those guns and move over against that side wall. *Or else he dies*. He dies and you got *nothing*. You got five seconds to make up your mind."

Eliot lowered his automatic until it hung beside his leg. Then he let go of it. As it clattered on the floor he whispered without moving his lips, "You're the marksman."

Stone gave no sign of having heard. Rudensky told him harshly, "I am not kidding you. Five seconds. *One* ...*two*..."

With an angry grimace, Stone tossed his gun away to his left. Rudensky's eyes automatically flicked to follow its curving fall. Stone whipped Malone's gun from his belt and fired.

The bullet missed Walter Payne's head by not much more than an inch. Rudensky toppled with a hole where his right eye had been. A last, convulsive tightening of his arm around Payne's neck dragged the bookkeeper to the floor with him.

Twisting desperately away from the dead man's arm, Payne rolled off his body onto his hands and knees. One hand came to rest on Rudensky's fallen revolver. He stumbled to his feet holding it pointed at Eliot and Stone.

"Let me go," he whispered shakily. "I...I..."

"Mr. Stone," Eliot said quietly without looking away from Payne and the gun in Payne's hand, "please go away now."

Stone hesitated and then obeyed. Backing out the doorway, he stopped on the platform where he could still see inside.

Eliot smiled gently at Payne and spread his hands a bit, showing them empty and unthreatening. He began to speak in a low, soothing monotone. "Mr. Payne, as of this instant you will consider yourself in federal custody. We have a lot of work to do, you and I, to prepare for your trial testimony. I'm going to save the questions until we get to my office."

Taking a slow step toward Payne, he continued in the

same level, reasonable tone. "I think you are doing the right thing, Mr. Payne. I think you're *much* safer with us than with Capone. Don't you agree, Mr. Payne? But we will protect you from them—and see that you come safe to trial."

Eliot moved closer, holding out his hand matter-of-factly for the revolver. "Mr. Payne? And so it's *over* for today."

Payne, a dazed expression on his face, gave Eliot the revolver.

Eliot thanked him politely and glanced at Stone as he came back in. "Mr. Stone, would you please take Mr. Payne to the car. And get it off the tracks, so the train can proceed on its way."

Stone started to take a pair of handcuffs from his pocket. Eliot stopped that with a shake of his head. "I don't think the handcuffs are necessary. Do you, Mr. Payne?"

After Stone took Payne's arm and led him out, Eliot walked to a bench and sat down. Looking at the revolver he'd taken from Payne, he put it down carefully beside him. Then he got out a cigarette.

But he discovered he couldn't light it. His hands were shaking too much.

THIRTY-ONE

It was on the third day of the trial that the prosecution came to the crucial point in the presentation of its case against Alphonse Capone.

District Attorney Morgan, having just handed up one of Walter Payne's ledgers to the presiding judge, Brian McClure, picked up another. He carried it to Payne, who was on the witness stand.

"And this ledger, Mr Payne—is this, like the previous one presented in evidence, one of the books in which you personally kept accounts of Mr. Capone's secret business transactions?" The D.A. handed the book to Payne.

Payne opened it, glanced at its pages, handed it back. "Yes," he said in a low voice, "that's what it is." He didn't look in Capone's direction when he said it. So far he had never once done so. Payne couldn't bring himself to meet Capone's stare.

"And do the coded entries in this ledger," the D.A. asked Payne, "represent cash disbursements to all levels of city officials, members of the police—and to Al Capone?"

"That is correct," Payne answered.

District Attorney Morgan looked at the judge and then at the jury, giving the answer time to sink in. "Excuse me, Mr. Payne," he said, still looking at the jury, "will you please speak louder, so we can hear you?"

Payne brought his voice up a bit. "I said that is correct."

Eliot, seated with Stone at the prosecution bench, glanced across the courtroom at Capone and didn't like what he saw. Capone, sitting between his chief defense attorney and Frank Nitti, looked as impassive as he had since the trial had begun. If his bookkeeper's testimony troubled Capone, he showed no sign of it.

Frowning, Eliot returned his attention to Walter Payne.

The D.A. was speaking to Payne again. "And you will decipher these coded entries for us?"

"I will," Payne said.

"You were in charge of disbursements for Mr. Capone?"

"I was."

"And you personally distributed monies—vast, undeclared monies—to Mr. Capone?"

Payne rubbed a hand across his mouth, dropped it to his lap, looked down at it.

"Mr. Payne?" the D.A. prodded firmly.

Payne raised his head. "Yes," he said finally. "I did."

Stone, looking toward the defense table, nudged Eliot and whispered, "I don't understand it—what's Capone got in reserve? We're nailing his coffin on him, and he sits there *smiling*."

Eliot looked over and saw that Capone was, indeed, smiling. And he no longer appeared to be paying any attention at all to Payne's testimony against him. Capone's smiling interest was on a sheet of paper he had in his hand.

Nodding, Capone folded the paper and gave it to Frank Nitti. Getting to his feet, Nitti tucked the folded paper in his pocket as he turned to leave.

The movement gave Eliot a brief glimpse of something under Nitti's jacket: a revolver in a shoulder holster. Then Nitti was strolling away toward the rear of the courtroom.

Eliot stood up quickly and hurried to a court bailiff. "That man's been wearing a gun in court!"

Nitti had closed the door of the courtroom behind him and was crossing the busy hallway outside when Eliot and the bailiff caught up to him.

"Just a minute," the bailiff snapped at Nitti. "Hold it right there."

Nitti stopped and looked at them. "What the hell . . .?"

"I want to check something Mr. Ness just told me about you." The bailiff pointed at a side door, his other hand resting on the butt of the gun holstered on his hip. "In private."

Nitti's cold eyes slid from the bailiff to Eliot. He shrugged and walked with them through the door into an empty corridor where a table stood against one wall across from the bottom of a narrow stairway. "Okay," he said in a bored tone, "what *is* this?"

Eliot grabbed Nitti's shoulder and spun him against the wall hard. Before he could recover from the suddenness of it, Eliot had the revolver out of Nitti's shoulder holster, showing it to the bailiff.

"Well, now." The bailiff drew his own gun and pointed it at Nitti. "Empty your pockets. Let's see what else you're carrying."

Nitti straightened his tie and got his bored expression back in place. "Hey, I got a *permit* to carry a gun."

"Not in court you don't. I said empty your pockets. On the table here. *All* your pockets."

Looking more bored than ever, Nitti began dumping things from his pockets onto the table. One of the last items he drew out was a large business card. Nitti looked at it and got a thin smile. "Here's something even *better'n* a permit." He handed the card to the bailiff.

Taking it, the bailiff looked uncomfortable as he registered the mayor's seal on it.

"Look at the other side," Nitti advised him.

The bailiff turned the card over and read what was written there, aloud: "To whom it may concern: Please extend to the bearer, Mr. Frank Nitti, all possible courtesy and consideration. Signed: Wm. Thompson, Mayor, City of Chicago."

The bailiff sighed and returned the card to Nitti. "Let him have his gun back," he told Eliot, and reholstered his own.

Eliot turned away in frustrated anger and dropped the gun on the table, got out a cigarette, and searched his pockets for matches. Not finding any, he picked up a matchbook dumped with Nitti's other possessions on the table. He tore out a match, but then didn't strike it. He was staring, transfixed, at something scrawled in pencil inside the matchbook: "1634 Racine."

The bailiff was reaching past him to pick up Frank Nitti's gun when Eliot turned around, repeating the address out loud. "You know," he told Nitti, "I had a *friend* who used to live there. And *this* makes you the one that's wanted for murdering him."

It was something Nitti saw in Eliot's eyes, more than the piece of evidence in his hand, that panicked him into what he did next. A gut reaction, too strong and sudden to allow time for cool thought.

He bolted up the narrow stairway.

Eliot brushed the bailiff aside and raced up the steps after him.

The bailiff, still holding Nitti's gun, remained frozen where he was and watched the two of them disappear around the turn at the top of the stairway, torn between Eliot's charge against Nitti and the mayor's endorsement of him.

Frank Nitti came up out of the top flight of steps through a door that opened onto the domed roof of the courthouse. He was breathing painfully from the speed of the climb that had kept him ahead of his pursuer. Gulping air into his heaving lungs, Nitti began to circle around the dome as fast as he could go, seeking a door through which he could descend via a different stairway.

In his haste, he tripped over some equipment left on the roof by a work crew repairing the dome. Scrambling back onto his feet, Nitti looked back. Eliot was coming around the dome after him. He wasn't running now, just advancing at a steady walk. He had already spotted what Nitti discovered after running farther along the roof: there was no other door to go down through. Only the one they'd both come out of. The man stalking Nitti slowed his advance, prepared to double back and cut Nitti off from that one exit door if he tried circling the dome to it.

Nitti came to a halt on the other side of the roof. The work crew had left a scaffold there. Hooked to one end of it was a block and tackle from which a long rope dangled down the side of the building. Leaning over the edge of the roof, Nitti saw a balcony jutting out below the end of the rope. It looked to him to be a short drop from the rope to that balcony.

He glanced back again. Eliot Ness was coming on toward him, his face expressionless. Nitti leaned out farther, tested his weight on the top end of the rope. Gripping it tightly with both hands, he swung off the roof and began to shimmy down.

It was a difficult climb for a man not used to that kind of exertion, but he made it to the bottom end of the rope

—only to discover that the perspective from the roof above had been deceiving.

The balcony was narrower than he'd thought, and much farther below the rope end. Too far to risk the drop. If he struck the balcony's railing it would snap his spine. If he missed it entirely, it would be a very long fall, the rest of the way below it, before hitting the pavement.

Looking up, he saw Eliot leaning over the roof's edge, gazing down at him impassively. Nitti's hands, arms, and shoulders were hurting now from the strain of his weight on the rope. But the aching pain helped him make his choice. It cut through the panic that had driven him to flee, and cleared his brain for sensible thought.

He'd been a fool to run, Nitti realized. He had nothing to fear from the law. It had gotten evidence against him before, often enough, and always in the end had to let him go.

He began climbing back up the rope. That proved a great deal harder than coming down. His aching muscles began to quiver, his hands getting weaker with each slow, painful pull, his body seeming to grow steadily heavier. By the time he neared the roof edge he was gasping, all of him trembling with exhaustion.

Clinging to the rope with one hand and his locked-together ankles, Nitti reached with his other hand for the ledge on which Eliot stood. The hand caught it, gripped it with all the strength remaining in it. Then, taking a shuddering breath, he let go of the rope and grabbed for the ledge with his other hand.

The hand missed its goal—and suddenly all of Frank Nitti's weight was hanging from the roof by that single, weakening hand.

His other hand flailed upward desperately, trying to catch hold of the ledge. And failed.

Eliot Ness crouched down on the edge of the roof,

crossing his forearms on his knees, looking down woodenly at the dangling Nitti.

The Enforcer hung helplessly by the one hand, looking up at Eliot, his mouth wide open and his eyes bulging. And there came into those eyes something no one had ever seen in them before.

Frank Nitti was silently pleading for his life.

Eliot continued to crouch there, watching him, no response at all in his expression.

The last vestige of power drained from Nitti's hand. His grasping fingers slipped.

In that last second, both of Eliot's hands caught hold of Nitti's wrist, gripping it tightly. Straightening, Eliot hauled him up and dropped him sprawling on the roof.

For a time Nitti remained that way, half sitting, staring at the solid roof under his braced hands, panting. Eliot stood over him, drawing a pair of handcuffs from his pocket. "On your feet. Hands behind your back."

Nitti slowly raised his hands from the roof surface, straightening himself up but remaining seated a bit longer, getting his breathing back to normal.

"On your *feet*," Eliot repeated.

Nitti gave it a few more seconds. Taking the time to compose himself, regain his cool. When he did stand up he had his bored expression back in place. Turning with a display of indifference, he put his arms behind him.

Eliot locked the cuffs on Nitti's wrists and shoved him toward the roof door. "They're going to *burn* you, thug. And I'm going to come and see you burn, you sonofabitch. You killed my friend."

"He died like he lived," Nitti said softly, viciously, "like a pig."

Eliot grabbed his shoulder, stopping him. *"What?"* It was more a gasp than a word.

Nitti looked back at Eliot over his shoulder with cold contempt. "I said your friend died screaming like an Irish pig. Think about *that* when you watch me beat the rap." Nitti twisted his shoulder out of Eliot's grasp and began to saunter toward the door.

The sound that welled up out of Eliot's throat was something no one had ever heard from him, and that no one would have recognized. He was not aware of making that sound; not aware of anything except the pressure of his blood inside his skull. He leaped forward and grabbed Nitti by his collar and belt and ran him to the edge of the roof.

And Nitti, being rushed inexorably toward the emptiness beyond, also let out a sound no one had ever heard from him before.

He screamed in horror.

And went on screaming after Eliot threw him off the roof—all the way down. Until he slammed into the roof of a parked car. It caved in under the impact, enfolding his mangled corpse a like twisted metal cradle.

THIRTY-TWO

Eliot came down the narrow stairway very slowly, pausing every few steps as though unsure of his balance.

Stone was in the corridor at the bottom, beside the bailiff, unfolding a sheet of paper he'd found among the items from Nitti's pockets still scattered on the table.

"Did you catch up with him?" the bailiff asked Eliot.

Eliot just stared at him, dazed. He felt numbed by what he had just done, incapable of thought or feeling.

Stone turned from the table. "I think you'd better see this, Mr. Ness."

Eliot didn't respond, still in another world.

"You'd better see this," Stone repeated, thrusting the unfolded sheet of paper into his hand.

Eliot made himself look at it. There was a list of names. Beside each name was written a sum of money. The amounts varied, ranging from a low of $1,500 up to $6,000.

Eliot made an effort to concentrate, not fully registering what it meant. "What is it?"

"It's the jury list," Stone told him. "They've been bribed."

Half an hour later, Judge McClure, having called a short recess, sat behind the desk in his chambers comparing the sheet of names and sums with his own list of the jurors in the Capone trial.

The U.S. district attorney stood before the desk, waiting anxiously for the judge's decision. Eliot Ness, standing against the wall near the closed door, watched the judge with narrowed eyes. He had shaken off the lethargy that had enveloped him after what he had done on the courthouse roof. But he was very pale; and something that had been part of him all his life was gone, perhaps forever. Something else had taken its place, but he couldn't be sure yet what it was, except that it was not something pleasant.

The judge looked up from the two lists and shook his head. "This constitutes no evidence," he told the district attorney. "It has no provenance, and I'm not about to—"

"Your Honor," Ness interrupted in a quiet but unyielding voice, "the *truth* of the case is that that man Capone is a killer and he will go free unless we do whatever has to be done, right now, to prevent it."

He walked forward until he was beside the desk, looking down at Judge McClure. "There is only one way to deal with such men and that is to *hunt them down*. I have . . ." Eliot's voice began to tremble. He took a deep breath and resumed in a slow, unwavering tone. "I have forsworn myself, I have . . . broken every law that I swore to defend. I have become what I beheld, and I am content that I have done right. Now, *that man must be stopped*, and you must—"

Judge McClure cut in angrily, "I think I'll be the judge of what I *must* do, Mr. Ness."

Eliot looked at the district attorney. "Will you excuse us?"

Worried, not understanding, the D.A. looked questioningly from Eliot to the judge.

"Your Honor," Eliot said, "I have something to tell you that I am certain you would not wish a third party to hear."

The judge hesitated, trying to read the expression—or lack of it—in Eliot's face. Finally he nodded.

The D.A. left the judge's chambers with a final worried, puzzled look at Eliot Ness.

Ten minutes later Judge McClure resumed his place on the bench, rapping his gavel sharply as the bailiff ordered everyone in the courtroom to take their assigned seats. The district attorney looked inquiringly at Eliot returning to the prosecution table. But Eliot sat down next to him without saying anything.

"Bailiff," the judge called.

The bailiff stepped forward. "Yes, sir?"

"Matters have come to my attention which necessitate a change before this trial may proceed. I want you to go next door to Judge Hoffman's court, where they are preparing to hear a divorce action. I want you to bring that jury here, and take *this* jury to his court."

The district attorney, stunned, turned to Eliot and whispered, "What on earth did you tell him?"

"I told him *his* name is listed in one of those coded ledgers, too."

"But his name isn't in any of them."

Eliot said, "The evil flee where no man pursueth."

"Bailiff," the judge was saying loudly, "are those instructions clear?"

The bailiff hurried over to the jury box and motioned for the jurors to file out. As they started to do so, Capone, who had taken several moments to believe what was happening to him, jumped to his feet shouting, "Hey! *Wait* a second!"

His chief defense counsel tried to pull Capone back

into his seat and hush him. Capone knocked his hand aside, yelling at the judge, "I said wait a second! What *is* this? Is this *the law*? What's going *on* here?"

His attorney stood quickly, clutching at Capone's arm again to silence him. "I think that we have to—"

"I don't care what you think," Capone fumed, turning on him furiously. "*Do* something here.... What am I? Do something!"

His attorney whispered to him urgently, "If we try to fight this they'll just add jury tampering to their other charges against you, Al. And *that* would add more years to your sentence. Our only chance is to throw ourselves on the mercy of the court—and try to make a deal."

Capone started to snarl something at him, but then just gaped at him as it sank in.

The defense attorney turned from him to address the judge. "Your Honor, we would like to withdraw our plea of not guilty and enter a plea of guilty."

Abruptly there was pandemonium in the courtroom as spectators began shouting and reporters rushed out to phone the news to their papers. Judge McClure began banging his gavel for order. He had to keep banging it again and again.

Al Capone sank down in his seat, still trying to cope with the enormity of what was suddenly happening to him. He pulled a handkerchief from his pocket and was dabbing sweat from his face when he became aware of someone standing nearby, looking down at him. Raising his head, Capone found himself looking up at an expressionless Eliot Ness.

Eliot nodded at him. "Never stop fighting till the fight is over. Here endeth the lesson."

And with those parting words, Eliot Ness turned away and walked out of the court.

Al Capone, choking on his own bile, could only stare after him.

THIRTY-THREE

On the day that the trial of Al Capone ended, Eliot Ness went to his office for the last time and packed a few items to take back with him to Washington. One of them was the front page of that morning's newspaper. Its banner read: CAPONE SENTENCED TO ELEVEN YEARS.

Eliot cut it from the paper and added it to the other souvenirs in his briefcase—including the two cartoons of him as a "crusader." The last thing he took from his desk was a photograph. It was the one Ferguson had taken of him, Wallace, Stone, and Malone under the wing of the Ford Tri-Motor airplane, all of them still in the sheepskin coats they'd worn during their battle with the Capone mob at the Canadian border.

He was looking at it when stone came into his office, dressed in his police academy recruit uniform.

"Playing hooky from school?" Eliot asked as he put the photograph into his briefcase.

Stone shrugged awkwardly. "Just wanted to say good-bye."

Eliot shut the briefcase and dug something out of his pocket, holding it out to Stone. "Here, I think this should be yours."

Stone looked at it: Malone's key-chain medallion. he started to reach out for it and then drew his hand back, though it was obvoius he wanted it. "Malone would have wanted *you* to have it."

"He would have wanted a *cop* to have it—a Chicago cop. And I'm going home." Eliot put into Stone's hand.

Stone held it for a moment and then put in his own pocket. "Thank you."

"Thank *you*. And —good-bye."

They shook hands, looking at each other, remembering.

"Good-bye, Mr. Ness."

Eliot smiled, picked up his briefcase, and walked past Stone, out of the office.

Stone remained behind for a bit, loking at the desk next to Eliots—the one that had been Malone's.

Coming out of the headquarters building, Eliot found a reporter waiting for him on the sidewalk. Only one. Of course it was Ferguson.

"Any comment for the record?" Ferguson asked him.

Eliot shook his head.

"Just a few words—from the man who put Al Capone on the spot?"

"There were a few others who had more to do with that," Eliot told him. "I just happened to be here in town when the wheel went around."

He started past Ferguson. The reporter gestured to stop him. "Just one more question, Mr. Ness. They say they're going to repeal Prohibition. What will you do then?"

"I think," Eliot told him with a smile, "I'll have a drink."

And with that he walked on, down the street.

Al Capone emerged from prison a sick shadow of former self. He died with his brain and body eroded by the syphilis that has begun eating at him years before, when he began his career as a whorehouse bouncer. But the example he set for other men like him did not die. Though Prohibition was repealed in 1933, the organized crime it spawned continues to grow, spreading its corrupting tentacles into every aspect of the American way of life today.